PRAISE FOR *Nothing Burns as Bright as You*

"*Nothing Burns as Bright as You* is a beautiful exploration of
first love with the emotional resonance that only an Ashley
Woodfolk novel can bring. Exquisite from beginning to end."
—ANGIE THOMAS, #1 *New York Times* best-selling author
of *The Hate U Give*

"*Nothing Burns as Bright as You* is utterly captivating, brimming with
passion and heartbreak and the beautiful complexity of the human heart."
—NICOLA YOON, #1 *New York Times* best-selling author of
The Sun Is Also a Star and *Instructions for Dancing*

"Despite the abundance of books lauding the magic and glory of a first
romance, I've never seen one that unapologetically shows the more
challenging elements of falling—and staying—in love . . . until now. With
verse as lyrical, succinct, and impacting as a favorite love song, Ashley
Woodfolk takes us through the highs, lows, and in-betweens of human
connection. This book has completely transformed the way I think about
what it means to love unconditionally."
—NIC STONE, #1 *New York Times* best-selling author of *Odd One Out*

"Wildly ambitious, fearlessly honest, and crackling with the
top volume feelings of messy first love. Ashley Woodfolk
is a virtuoso. Consider my breath fully taken."
—BECKY ALBERTALLI, #1 *New York Times* best-selling author
of *Simon vs. the Homo Sapiens Agenda* and *Leah on the Offbeat*

"This highly original story is both heart-wrenching and hopeful. Ashley
Woodfolk takes chances with form that make this verse novel captivating.
Her skill as a writer has never burned so bright. Pure fire!"
—KWAME ALEXANDER, *New York Times* best-selling author

"There is something sacred in the way Woodfolk bears witness to the scariest, most vulnerable parts of an untamable heart. A fierce, wrenching, deeply honest look at first love—I invite Ashley Woodfolk to break my heart with a book like this anytime."
—LEAH JOHNSON, author of the Stonewall Honor book *You Should See Me in a Crown*

"*Nothing Burns as Bright as You* consumed me like a flame. The interspersed timelines will keep readers breathless as the love between these girls splatters raw on the page, the poetry absolute perfection. A novel to at once devour and savor."
—KIP WILSON, author of *White Rose*

"A loving ode to the queer twin flame relationships of our adolescence that smolder quietly in so many of us. These characters, like Woodfolk's dazzling and soulful lyrical prose, are both limitless and full of complexity. An exhilarating and quixotic read."
—JUNAUDA PETRUS, author of the Coretta Scott King Honor book *The Stars and the Blackness Between Them*

Nothing Burns as Bright as You

Nothing Burns as Bright as You

ASHLEY WOODFOLK

Versify
An Imprint of HarperCollinsPublishers

For you
(and me)

The cure for anything is salt water — sweat,
tears, or the sea.

— Karen Blixen

What matters most is how well you walk through
the fire.

— Charles Bukowski

AFTER THE FIRE

I'd been running away from everything for years,
my body like the flame of a lit match,
tip touched to a line of gasoline.
But this was the first time I'd turned to look back.

You were right where I'd left you,
stooped and steadfast,
at the opposite end of the bridge between us:
as lovely and as luminous as you'd ever been.

You still seemed desperate and devoted too,
but you were not coming after me.
You were not even looking in my direction.
And I wondered at this change in you.

Had you broken an unspoken promise between us?
(That where I went, you would follow.)
Or had I finally shattered something that had been cracked
and slowly splintering since the day we met?

I was used to absence. I was used to being alone.
But I'd also grown too used to you.

I wept as I waited for you to glance up.
Struggled to catch my breath as I silently urged
those dark eyes of yours to find me in the early morning light.

I clung to my own fingers, hoping you'd say something,
anything,
that would make me turn around and come back.

You never looked for me.
(Or maybe you were tired of always looking for me.)
You didn't fight for me this time.
You let me go.
So I went.

I love you. I think you know I will always love you.

But maybe I'll let you start
from the beginning.

867 DAYS BEFORE THE FIRE

You ordered the same drink as me
and you used the same fake name.
Grande skinny caramel macchiato Frappuccino,
for Alex?
And our soft brown hands collided
like stars.

1. Opposites

You think it'll be funny
to start a fire.
You always thought starting fires was funny.
Whether they were real, like the way you'd write down wishes
and set the pages ablaze in your backyard,
or less than real, like the endless fights you started with me
(only with me).

Fire was always a joke.
And matches burned holes in your pockets
the way money burned through mine.

You'd started fires on street corners and under bridges.
In empty alleyways and at the ends of joints lifted and held steady,
our eyes locked and loaded before we smoked.
This time, though, feels different.
Dangerous.
This time, you want flames to fill the dumpster in the school's back
    lot.

The joke, you say the night before we do it,
is that this whole year has been a dumpster fire.
And what better way to celebrate it ending
than with a literal dumpster that's literally on fire?

I thought it would be better
to flood the back lot instead.
Less obvious, I insist.
Easier to get away with.
Because water could be accidental
in a way arson could not.

Pipes burst.
Tides ebb.
Sewers get blocked by fallen leaves.
Things leak and overflow sometimes
just because it's a thing things do.

(But combustion is only very rarely spontaneous.)

I could imagine the miniature disasters that might follow a
     flood —
Ant-sized tsunamis.
Tiny tidal waves.
A slippery, perilous surface to cross
if it was cold enough.

It's a metaphor, I say. *Because we're all under water.*
Either swimming
or drowning.

But you aren't into it.

And this
is a perfect metaphor
for us:
Fire and water. Flames and frost.
Hot and cold, burning and freezing.
Opposites.

You never could get the heat of your body
(your temper like tinder,
your being wanting to burn)
under control.
But I like it when you are in control.

I always want to be close to the inferno of you,
even if it kills me.

A lie:

"Opposites attract."

The truth?
Magnets attract.
Opposites fit together like (fucked up) puzzle pieces.

And when you're fucked up, there are more important things than
    attraction.

                    Like distraction. Like destruction.

Opposites distract.
Opposites destroy.
Opposites decimate.
Opposites detonate.

Opposites are fun as hell,

               until they aren't.

703 DAYS BEFORE THE FIRE

You took me to your basement room.

It was filled with mismatched furniture:
wrought iron chairs and
two cushy couches and
a four-poster bed with a princess canopy.
Nothing went together.
So everything did.

You sleep down here? I asked.
Yessss, you said, teeth hissing like burning paper.

There were patchwork quilts and
concert posters.
Christmas lights and
an aquarium shimmering with fish.
Sunshine-yellow sheets and
piles of books and
so many candles.

There was a rainbow painted across the floor instead of a carpet.
Gay, I whispered, looking down at all the colors we stood atop.
You laughed.
Yep, you said, lips popping like firecrackers.

I could see you in that bed,
under the low ceiling covered in glow-in-the-dark stars,
lying awake above the rainbow.
Making wishes. Setting tiny fires.
Reading poetry and texting me back with your dark hair
bleeding across your bright pillow.

It looked like a dream, your basement.
It looked like the best kind of secret.
It looked like home.

And I imagined it was what your brain might look like
if I could see inside you the way I wanted.

2. The best fire starters

The forecast is ice cold the next day
and you have a theory that things burn hotter,
longer,
brighter,
in this kind of weather.
I don't question you
(I rarely ever question you),
so we decide to do it.

It is also the winter solstice, I realize
when my alarm goes off in the deep morning dark,
and something about setting a fire
before the sun rises
on the shortest day
and longest night of the year
feels holy.
Or blasphemous.
Or maybe a bit of both.

I leave my house without making a sound
to collect dozens of city papers from doorsteps
and front lawns while the sun is still deciding to show up.
When I have enough, I head to school.
And once I'm standing in front of the dumpster,
I pull apart the sections,
layering them inside
like the colors in the early morning sky.

You meet me there, in the back lot,
and when I see you coming
I yank my hat lower to hide more of my eyes.

I thought if I saw less of you, you'd see less of me.

                                  (Less of how I ache to touch you.)
                                  (Less of how badly I need you close.)

But you're too difficult to look away from.

Your wild hair is pulled back
in a way that makes me want to set it free.
Your hands are stuffed into your pockets,
your face half-hidden inside a big scarf.
You hate the cold and I love it,
but I love you more.
So always, even in winter, I pray for heat.

I want to reach for your hair and your hands and your face.
I want to shield you from the bitter wind
and everything else.
To look at you for hours or days or as long as you'd allow.
But we have things to do.

So I laugh
(as I usually do when the wanting is too much)
and say, *You ready?* instead.

You look sleepy but excited,
your eyes full of brightness even in the dark.
Your nervous energy, your grin, your quick nod
are pleasure-punches in the chest:
shots of adrenaline to my already racing heart.

I tear the paper's movie listings and book reviews to pieces
and let them flutter down — black and white confetti.
Words like *action-packed* and *unputdownable*
blanket the trash in the dumpster,
and I can already see sparks.

The best fire starters know
a fire needs to have layers.
Like a sundae, I heard you say once.
Like . . . a parfait.

So I twirl,
lift my hands high,
wait for the wind to settle.

I add even more.

You call me an artist as the pile of debris and trash grows.
I say,
Someone once told me that starting a fire
is a kind of art.
(That someone was you.)

I learned everything I know about making things burn bright
from your quick, quiet hands.
So maybe the art was in the way you saw me:
As someone special.
As someone other than exactly who you'd made me.

The sports and local news sections come next.
You crumple the gray pages into loose balls and shoot fadeaways
        until none are left.
Then we lose our patience
(or maybe we're worried about losing our nerve)
and finish up, fast.
We add sticks and leaves
and other nearby, burnable things because
the sun is quickly rising, chasing away the dark.

School will start soon,
so we need to get gone
and the fire needs to already be burning.

When we sneak back,
we'll widen our eyes and cover our mouths.
We'll laugh and point and gasp,
looking innocent and astonished
just like everyone else.

You flick your lighter open.

You wanna do the honors? you ask.

I say yes only because I need to stare at something,

anything,

brighter than you.

The sun's still not quite in session.

So I settle for the flames.

515 DAYS BEFORE THE FIRE

I took you to the beach because you'd never been.

When you stepped out of the car and saw the ocean for the first
    time,
as wide and as seamless as a rippling blue blanket,
you looked at me like I'd personally knit together something
you'd only seen before in dreams.

The water was cold,
the way it always is on our coast.
But the sand, it burned.

I swam and you sat, reading, sinking your hands into the hot,
    salt-soaked earth.
Then we lay out, side by side on thick dark towels.
The sun shined right into our squinting eyes,
and for a while, we didn't care.

I told you a story about my brother,
how he had called me Doll when I was small.
You told me your sister called you Devil back then
and sometimes she still did, even now.
We shaded our eyes so we could each see the other's grin.

When I complained about the brightness,
about having to close my eyes,
about not being able to see you,
you sat up fast.

You scooted forward,
leaned over, closer and closer to me,
until you (and all your hair) blotted out the sun completely.

I'll be your shade, you said.
Open your eyes.

And something deep in my chest quivered
when I looked up at you, haloed in light.

You were something heavenly.
You were something on fire.

Because like your shadow,
your singularity and wonder and kindness
were beginning to blot out
all the mediocrity and meanness
that had been blinding me
for years.

I was starting to see something.
(About the world. About us.)
But I didn't yet know
what.

A truth:

We were
best
friends.

3. More of you

I rode my bike to the lot
so that, on the off chance they noticed,
I wouldn't have to explain a missing car
to my nosy parents.

I throw my blue ten-speed
into your hatchback,
the fire growing like a second sunrise
in the rearview mirror
as we laugh and slam our heavy doors.

Holy shit, you say,
your breath a cloud, even as your loud vents
blast hot air onto our cold faces.
You toss your arm across the back of the passenger seat as you
    back up,
and take off.
And I can smell you —
something sweet, burning.

Holy shit, I repeat.
(But really,
in that moment
your scent,
your arm,

and the proximity of you to the blushing skin
on the back of my neck
are the only holy things I've been close to in months.)

*   *   *

The road from school to your house is still
dawn-dim and pretty;
the trees on either side
are shadowed soldiers waiting for the command to attack.
I stare through my window,
still aching with want,
and decide I can't take it anymore.

Pull over here, I say,
because I don't want to sit in your driveway,
in my aching skin,
for the ninety minutes left before first bell.

I can't imagine going home
when it is so early and you are so close.
You set me on fire
while I sent something else up in flames,
and the only thing that will put me out now
is you.

More of you.

You listen.
I watch your long brown fingers,
your shimmering pink nails,
as you make a sharp left,
your hands crossing, dancing
over the wheel to maneuver us into position.

Then tree-soldiers are the only witnesses
as I maneuver myself out of my seat belt,
out of my seat,
and into yours.

Your eyes are dark and playful
and still just waking up,
the same way the city looks from where we sit
on this hill,
in your car.
You tug away my hat,
running your hands over my short, shorn hair
at the same time as I shove my fingers
into your fat, frizzy curls.

Hey, you say.
Oh, hey, I say back.

I hug you
(because I love to hug you),
hold you so close and tight.

Let the heat zip from my belly button
lower.
Fill me up like darkness at night.

I touch your forehead,
your cheek,
your plump bottom lip.
Then you grab on to mine with your easy, white teeth.
You kiss me,
and I hold my breath.
Hold any and every thing I can reach.

We do this sometimes now
ever since we decided we could:

It's okay if we say more than friends would say.

I love you. I need you. I want you.

It's okay if we touch more than friends would touch.

Hands in hair. Cheeks on bellies. Lips on lips on lips.

It's okay if we do more than friends would do.

And I knew it might confuse someone else
if their best friend suddenly straddled them on the side of the road
after they'd made a mutual mess of their reputations

(and maybe their permanent records)
a few days before winter break.

But somehow
it made a messy kind of sense
to us.

437 DAYS BEFORE THE FIRE

First, we held hands.
Just once, but once was enough.

The way your fingers made mine feel right and warm.
The quick zing of something electric between our palms.
The way, when you let go, it felt like
something precious had just been stolen from me.
And how, whenever I did,
you'd pout and steal my hand right back.

A few weeks later,
when you laid your head
(and all that gorgeous hair)
on my shoulder,
I thought I'd never breathe the same way again.

And within a month
we'd curved around each other on one of your cushy couches
like double commas:

> A typo.
> A poetic mistake.

*   *   *

When we kissed for the first time,
it didn't feel the way I thought it would.

There was no kaleidoscope
of butterflies in my chest.
No bursts of colorful fireworks
behind my still-shut eyes.
No heat in my cheeks or
confusion about where my hands
should land.

It just felt right.
Like sun on sea-wet hair.
Like paint spread thick and bright on canvas.
Like lying in grass, the spiky chill of the blades against my arms,
the warm breeze of the day, a soft breath across my face.

My eyes trained on the sky, staring at clouds, and spotting one
suddenly
that holds the shape of a poem;
the one thing I needed to see
just long enough for me to see it.

*　*　*

Soon after that,
your hands became the only things I liked to hold.
Your eyes, the place I liked most to get lost.
Your thick thighs, a secret I whispered about in my sleep.

For every piece of you I wanted,
there was a piece of me you had to have back.
(But I wouldn't let myself believe it.)

You checkin' me out? you'd ask.
No, I'd lie.

Everything about you was
dark, gorgeous, and round:
a cluster of clouds filled with desire
instead of rain.

So yeah. I was checkin' you out.

I was studying you like a goddamn book.

You were a hurricane I couldn't help but wait for.
A wave I wanted to be swallowed by.
I was armed and ready to be overtaken by
the ocean of you.

There was only one problem:
preparation for a coming storm
won't save anyone
in a fire.

A lie (I kept telling myself):

"She will learn to love you well."

The truth?
You loved me the only way you knew how.

4. Come with me

Someone saw us.
It was probably that bitchy junior,
the one we stink bombed in September.
Or one of the many boys
(or girls)
whose advances we'd spurned
because we preferred each other
over everyone else.

Maybe it was a teacher.
A young, overachieving one,
who spotted your car in the back lot
(because they were in absurdly early)
or pulled over on the hill
(because they were on their way).

Your hatchback is nondescript enough
but your license plate isn't:
FLYIN HI.

Either way
we have enough enemies not to know who turned us in,
who may have witnessed our criminal activity.
(But luckily,
hopefully,
not the way we touched in the half-light
of the morning sun.)

You two, the vice principal says
as you park,
before I even completely open the passenger door.
Her hand is on her hip, and her perfect, permed hair
curls around her ear with as much attitude as her words
curl through the air.
In that moment I can tell
that outside of school walls
she's a "Mama," not a "Mom."

Come with me.

*   *   *

The fire is still raging and it's taller than the both of us by now.
Kids are gathered, hissing and whistling,
taking pictures and video.
And as we pass, a slow applause fills the air:
a rising crescendo that sounds like the inside of a seashell,
crashing waves of all the wrong kinds of respect.
But it's the kind we're used to.
The kind we are always chasing.

Hardcore, someone whispers.
I bite my lip. You smirk.
Badass, they say,
and it feels like a blessing.

But then the janitor runs out with a hose and a fire extinguisher
right before we reach the door.
The gathered crowd laughs as he
fights the fire with water
and then foam,
covering the dumpster
in a wet, white mess
until all that's left
is a smelly, smoking heap.

His gray jumpsuit will stink of burning trash for the rest of the day.

My pride turns to guilt
because he's old and nice.
No.
He's ancient and kind.
I look at you and I can see that you're thinking the same thing as
     me:
We didn't think about him.

Meet me in my office, the vice principal says as she veers off,
headed to the dumpster.
Maybe to check the wreckage.
Maybe to look for proof.
She leaves us standing there,
shaky and ashamed
on the front steps.

I swing the double doors of the school open wide.

Don't go anywhere except straight to
my office.

Her words rise white and foggy from her mouth,
solid and serious in the cold morning air
as she moves
farther and farther
away from us.

And I want to take it all back:
The fire.
The morning make-out session.
The way we are always together
but not.

I step inside.
You reach for my hand.
I take it.
Squeeze it once.

I let you go.

415 DAYS BEFORE THE FIRE

The first time we got into trouble at school,
it was my fault.

I collect things.
Strange and pretty and unusual things.
Weathered old coins.
Oddly shaped sea glass.
Translucent gemstones and opaque marbles,
pale feathers, skeleton keys, saffron-yellow flowers.

You're like a raven, you said,
the first time I showed you all my stuff.

How?

You're brilliant and brave and you hoard beautiful things,
you said, without even looking at me.
When you touched the small tokens like they were sacred,
I wanted to kiss your fingertips.

Most days I keep one with me:
My grandfather's old whiskey stones if I'm sad.
A piece of silk ribbon if I'm sick.
A folded love letter my dad wrote my mom
on the rare occasion I'm feeling optimistic.

Promises made real.
Blessings I can hold in my hands.
I let them rest deep in my pockets:
tiny, heavy secrets I share only with myself.

Sometimes I pieced them together into something new:
A seashell bracelet for my mother's delicate wrist.
A mosaic of coins for my brother's dorm room wall.
A crystalline marble with a hole drilled straight through it
strung with black leather and threaded between the pages
of my father's Bible.
A piece of me,
for the people I carried around in my heart,
made from something I had once carried around in my pockets.

And I wanted,
no, I *needed*
the rock our science teacher had on her desk.

It wasn't just any rock.
It was an opal.
A *contraluz opal,* she explained on the first day of tenth grade
as we all sat there,
bored and belligerent,
wanting to be elsewhere.

So what, someone muttered,
and everyone laughed.

Everyone but me.
I was staring at the rock.

It was heart-shaped and -sized
and held a whole galaxy inside it.
Colors and clouds and crystals,
like the sky and sea made solid
at once.

Seeing it felt like *my* heart was on display.
Because I was full of colorful feelings
as wide as the sky,
as deep as the sea,
as jagged as crystal,
as wispy as clouds.

You saw me see it.
Saw the naked need.
You didn't even blink when I said,
That rock's gotta be mine.
You just agreed.

We waited until the science teacher went on vacation.
Until we had a clueless sub for nearly a week.
And you just shoved it into your backpack
while I asked the sub a bunch of dumb,
distracting questions.

I hid it in a wooden box under my bed,

instead of putting it on my dresser

with the rest of my treasures.

Because hearts are meant to be felt,

known,

held with more tenderness than anything else in the world,

not seen.

(But hearts, real ones at least, can't be kept hidden for long.)

When the teacher got back

and saw that it was gone,

she immediately looked at me.

She must have noticed all the times I stared at it

like I was looking through a window.

Must have seen the love I had for it in my unblinking eyes.

She looked at you next,

because by then we were a set.

A left and right.

A yin and yang.

Two troublesome halves of a maddening whole.

But they couldn't raid your brain to prove that you'd taken it.

They couldn't come to my house to prove that I had it.

So they stared at us. Threatened us.

Questioned us together. Questioned us apart.

Told me you'd told them I'd done it.

Told you I'd told them you'd done it.

We never cracked, but they gave us detention anyway.

And all I could think about as I sat there refusing to break
was how *contraluz* meant "against the light"
and how, from then on, I knew
it would be you and me
against everything.

A truth:

Maybe, if we had been other,
different
people, we would have just dated.

I would have asked you out.
You would have said yes.
It would have been everything.

But I was me.
And you were you.
And my me-ness plus your you-ness
was an unbalanced equation.

There was something about each of us that was a little too empty
to handle the fullness that came from our
us-ness.

More simply put:
we added up to a little too much.

You loved me more than I knew.
I loved you more than you could take.

We talked about it constantly,
and then
(when it became clear that it was what it was,
we were who we were:
damaged, with missing pieces, but still whole enough to break
more)
we didn't talk about it at all.

5. Windowless room

Inhale.
Exhale.
Inhale.
Exhale.
I breathe deeply right before I have to tell the truth.
The burst of oxygen shocks my system
so I forget, however briefly,
that it would be easier for me to lie.

It was me, I say,
fingering a dark feather, thin as tissue paper, soft as silk,
in my pocket.
They know enough to know it was one of us
and I can't let them think it was you.
I did it, and she didn't. Punish me and let her go.

But it was my idea,
you say,
even as I mentally plead with you to shut up.
It was my idea, and I helped.

My father says the truth will set you free,
but for me, the truth is a windowless room.
It steals my breath, no matter how much air I collect before the
    telling.

Like diving headfirst into the deep end.
Like sticking my head out a car window
while my brother is driving too fast on the freeway.
Like missing the last stair and feeling like I'm falling,
even if the feeling only lasts
for less
than a second.

But when you squeeze my hand, I'm not falling anymore.
Or rather, I'm landing, sinking into place,
a head on the cool side of a pillow.

I don't care, the vice principal says.
I don't care whose idea it was.
Or who lit the match.
Or frankly which one of you wants to take the blame this time.
You've both been on thin ice all semester.
And unfortunately for you,
you were seen.
This is out of my hands.

She picks up her phone.
Says a few words.
Hangs up.
Stabs us with her dark eyes as she stands.

Stay here.

1,232 DAYS BEFORE THE FIRE

When I was thirteen
I almost died.

We were at the beach
and I was wearing a bikini (my first bikini).
It was the color of seashells,
the color of sand.
A not-quite-white that shone against my dark skin
like moonlight.

It was the year I let my hair get really long.
And it was one of the few times I let my mom do it.
Beads sat on the ends of my braids
like buoys on the ropes that split the ocean in half:
Here, it was safe to swim.

                                There, it wasn't.

My nails were painted too,
so my fingers and toes glittered in the sun,
making me feel full of something like light.
And no matter which way I walked or swam or moved,
it kept bursting from the tips of me,
bright and brilliant.

Girls are told their whole lives that what they wear matters.
Girls are taught that their looks can keep them out of

(or get them into)
trouble.
And girls, especially Black girls, learn that the way they look,
what other people think about their clothes or their hair or their
    bodies
("grown," "nappy," "*developed*"),
can put them in danger.

But I felt safe at the beach with my family.
I felt safe in my new swimsuit,
with fresh braids and painted nails.
I looked well taken care of —
spoiled even.
I felt safe because
I looked like someone loved me
and would notice if I was gone.

There was a cute girl building a sandcastle
and I thought I recognized her from school.
Her swimsuit was bright red with
blooming yellow flowers, and her hair was bushy,
but curly on the ends because it was a little wet.

I didn't know much about anything
(I was only thirteen),
but I knew I noticed the tiny flowers on her swimsuit
before I even saw the loud, sweaty boys playing volleyball behind
    her.

And I knew that meant something:
about what I liked,
about who I might someday love.

I didn't know what to do with that.

I was only thirteen, so I was thinking deeply about those feelings
(what they might mean, what people might think, how it might
    change everything)
when
He
came over.

I was a kid, and
He
wasn't, so
I treated him like a grown-up.
I listened to him. I trusted him.
He
was older than me, so
He
knew better than me.
(Right?)

I like your hair,
He
said. But
He
stared at every other part of me.

Thank you.

You know how to swim?
He
asked. But
He
wasn't watching the water.

Yes.

I have a toddler who is trying to learn.
He
pointed vaguely toward the shoreline,
where there were lots of little kids splashing.
Can you show her?

Okay.

I glanced back at where my parents were laid out on our blanket.
My dad was reading.
My mom was napping.
My brother was playing a game on his phone.
They didn't love the beach the way I did,
so I was used to hanging out in the sand and water alone.

We went out into the ocean and
He
couldn't find her.
Oh no,

43

He

said, spinning in a small circle.

She was right here.

And I felt a tight, urgent flutter in my chest,

imagining a tiny girl,

in tiny water wings, who couldn't swim,

who was missing.

I don't really know what

He

planned to do at that point.

After

He

lied.

Maybe convince me to search on another part of the beach.

Maybe ask me to look behind the big rocks

where older kids sometimes went to kiss.

Maybe

something

else.

But before

He

could try another one of his quick tricks,

I ducked away from him and dove.

I swam out, beyond the rope and buoys,

picturing a lost little girl.

I knew I wasn't supposed to be so far from shore.

But I knew how to swim

well and fast
and there was no time to waste.

Everything was blue.
That's the one thing I remember.
All around me, there was nothing but sky and sea,
so deep
and so everywhere,
all at once.

I think it hit me then, that
He
was a liar.
That there had been something sinister
hidden in his request.
And the thought that a grown-up man
would use a lie about a tiny girl
to trick a slightly less tiny one
made something inside me crack.

I swam harder and faster away from him.
And everyone else.
Thinking about how many lies I'd been told in my life.
Lies about tiny girls who I could teach to swim.
Lies about what I wore.
Lies about how to stay safe.
Lies about who I was supposed to want.
About who I was supposed to kiss.

I was about a half mile offshore when I opened my eyes
and thought that here was the only place I could go
to get away from all the lies.

It was so peaceful.
I felt safe again.
I didn't want to leave.

I stopped swimming.
I don't know why I stopped, but I stilled my arms and legs
and let myself float.
When I spotted a wave, big and brutal as a body-sized fist,
I didn't panic, because I knew how to swim.
I could save myself.

I took a deep breath. I went under.

I looked at my bright fingernails.
I looked at my beaded braids, which were floating around and in
     front of me,
my very own set of tentacles.
I loved feeling weightless,
and I wondered out of nowhere if this
blue peace
was what it would feel like, look like,
to die.
I closed my eyes as the wave hit
and it sent me spinning.

The next thing I remember is choking.
My throat burned and
I was puking up water and
my mother was wailing:
a siren song of fear.

My father was kneeling beside me in the sand,
his eyes scanning for help like the beam of a lighthouse,
and so much water was falling off my brother's face
and onto mine
that I didn't realize until later
that he was crying.

He hovered over me,
his dripping afro blocking out the sun
like a big, black cloud.

He saw me go under, but I never came back up.
He didn't even give me a chance to.

He said, *What the hell is wrong with you?*
even though our parents were right there
and *hell* was a swear word he should not have been using in front of
     them.

I said, *I didn't need to be rescued.*

The truth was, I didn't know what the hell was wrong with me.

Because nothing is wrong with me.

But it's hard to remember that,

to believe it,

in a world that always makes things that aren't your fault

your fault.

(Like my hair and my body.)

(Like that lying grown-up.)

(Like that wave.)

(Like the way I've always noticed pretty girls before any of the
     boys.)

(Like feeling sad without a "reason.")

Like every little thing that happens in the world that

we

          can't

                    stop.

A year later, almost to the minute,

I met you

and I'd felt helpless,

powerless,

for nearly four hundred days.

But when I told you this story,

you looked me in the eye

and said, with your always steady voice,

You were right.

You didn't need to be rescued.

You are infinitely powerful.

You had already saved yourself.

6. Good Kids™

We aren't Good Kids™.

We're the kids teachers always talk about having
"potential."
Because we're too smart for our own good.
But too devious for anyone else's.

Sometimes we do what people expect Good Kids™ to do:
we read piles of books and
are enthusiastic in class and
complete all our homework and
ace quizzes.

But we don't do any of it for the reasons Good Kids™ do,
so people don't "get" us.
(They didn't understand
me or you,
so they certainly don't understand
me-and-you.)

We're too different.
And no one
likes different.

We make the real Good Kids™ mad
just by being ourselves.

And when they get upset
(about things we say or do, clothes we wear, how little we care about
    everything),
we get mad right back.

We're too righteous to be bad
but too proud to let things slide.
Don't mess with us, we're always saying.
We won't let you get away with it.
We're weird, but guess what?
We won't take your shit.

Like
when that junior got mad I took her spot on the swim team
and she soaked my swimsuit in something that made it smell rancid.
You let me borrow yours
so I could still swim in the meet
and then set off a stink bomb in her locker.

Like
when that senior called you a cow when he thought no one was
    listening
and mooed softly whenever you walked past.
I told him to shut the fuck up,
gave him a bloody nose,
and covered his desk in a few pounds of raw beef the next day.
I left a note that read *Who's the cow now?*

Like

when the gym teacher gave girls a hard time about forgetting their
    shorts
but said nothing to the boys when they forgot theirs.
I called him a perv and you backed me up
and we got detention for a week.

We spent the wasted hours writing him hate letters,
folding them into elaborate origami hearts.

When we delivered one to him daily for the rest of the month,
other girls started doing it too.
Until the hallway in front of his office door was littered with
paper hearts and animals and flowers:
pretty hand-folded art full of
ugly handwritten truths.

So we aren't good.
And we aren't bad.
But we conform too little.
Do what we want too much.

If you'd told me high school was gonna be like this,
I wouldn't have believed you.

This whole year has been a dumpster fire, you said.
And I know it will get worse before anything gets any better.

                    *   *   *

The vice principal comes back.
A school officer is with her.

The officer steps forward first.
I reach for your hand again.

I'm guessing you meant no harm
since the dumpster is so far from the building?

It seems like he's trying to help us,
so I nod, hard.

You play with fire often? he asks next.
And finally, finally I can lie.

No, I say. *Never.*
It slides from my lips,
a soft sigh of relief.

He looks at you.

Never, I say again. Louder.

You guys seem like good kids, he says.
So we won't file a police report.

And you're lucky we were able to put it out quickly.
We didn't have to call the fire department.
They wouldn't have been so forgiving.

He looks at us both.
Shakes his head.
Don't let it happen again.

And I can't help but feel something indignant rise in me like the
    sun,
slow and distant but with enough heat to singe skin.

We didn't "let" this happen.
We did it on purpose. With purpose.
We were making a statement.
We were making a point.
And even when it's right in front of them,
they're missing it:

our lives
are on fire
and
no one
fucking
cares.

You squeeze my hand hard and rhythmic
like you can feel how all the words are
pulsing through me, begging to get out.
You replace that pulse with a new one
that says,
Shut up,

      shut up,

            shut up.

I look at our hands until my breathing slows.
I study your pink nail polish. My shredded cuticles.
Your chunky rings and the nearly invisible hairs growing out of my
    knuckles.
I grit my teeth.
Swallow my pride.

The vice principal crosses her arms.

You're suspended, she says.
For two weeks, for setting a fire on school grounds.
But unfortunately, that dumpster belongs to the city,
not to us.
Depending on the damage,
there could be legal action.
Misdemeanors.
Court.
She shakes her head, runs her hand over her face.
Runs her eyes over ours.
We'll have to wait and see.

I look at you.
You look at me.
And we both say,

Shit.

A lie:

"This will be on your permanent record."

The truth?
Nothing is permanent.

Not even you.

1,101 DAYS BEFORE THE FIRE

When you were thirteen
you believed you could fly.

You could.
And you often did.

You were a gymnast who
flew over blue-carpeted auditoriums
in a flurry of flips and jumps and kicks.

Winning over judges and crowds.
Winning medals and ribbons
every color of the rainbow.

(*Gay,* I said when I saw all of them on a shelf in your basement.
You'd arranged them ROY G BIV on purpose.
So gay, you said back.)

You were a thrill seeker who cut lines at fairs and carnivals and
    amusement parks
just to fly over the fastest, loopiest, scariest roller-coaster tracks,
your body held in place by only thin vinyl seat belts and nerve.

You were a passenger who always climbed into
the beds of pickup trucks
or hung out of moonroofs and windows,
your arms flung wide.

You flew over never-ending roads,
wind flinging your hair.
You were a boat
with a dark and curly set of sails.

You flew through books,
reading more in a week than some people did
in a year.

You were a girl
who flew into the arms of other girls
and boys
and anyone who fell for you,
and people fell for you like rain.
(But you almost never fell back.)

And then there was the burning of things
and how it made you feel like you were flying.
Or maybe it just makes me feel like a flame, you said.
Too hot and bright and dangerous
to touch or catch or kill.

So you trusted flying.
You trusted your arms and legs.
You trusted speed and blazing hot heat.
You trusted wind and will and wildness,
but never anyone else.

Until we met
and became
us.

You told me about all the ways you took flight
and I told you to take me with you.
That I was afraid of heights,
of doing anything too quickly,
of burning too brightly.
But you made me less afraid of everything.

So off we went.
Together we flew.
And I, like so many before me,
fell hard and fast for you.

It wasn't until you told me
that love felt like tripping,
felt like losing your balance,
felt inevitable, like a force of nature,
like gravity,
that I realized:

you never learned the difference between flying high
and
falling.

7. This closeness

When my brother pulls up in the back lot to pick me up,
he's leaning out the driver's side window,
shaking his head.
You two are a hot mess, he says.
But he smiles, because he loves us anyway.

He had his last final two weeks before Christmas
and his next semester won't start for nearly a month,
so when they called my house, he answered
and pretended to be Daddy so well
that they believed him.

I'll come collect them both right away, he tells us he said.
I'm very disappointed.
I don't know what has gotten into them.
Oh, we're extremely close with her family.
Don't worry if you can't reach them.
We'll handle it.

I've never been happier to see him.

You skip over and wrap your arms around his neck.
You say, *Mama's gonna kill us.*
Like she's your mother,
like he's your brother,

like his features are the same ones on your face
(but bigger, broader, a little less pretty)
and not mine.

Your hatchback is parked right beside his pickup,
but you abandon it so you can ride with us.

He just got his hair done.
So when we climb into the truck,
the whole cab smells of coconuts.
Some of his locs swing like vines
around his brooding brown face,
while others are interwoven:
dark macramé art hanging
on his head instead of on walls.

(Seeing his, I don't miss my hair at all.)

Fire, he says. Really?
And you bite your bottom lip.
I lean against the window,
staring at the still-smoldering dumpster,
and nod.

He plays something slow and melancholy
on the stereo
as he starts to drive,
and the song sounds the way my heart feels —
savage and braying and somber,

horses running, unbridled,
at night.

What is this music? you ask.
It sounds like what's inside me.
And I have to swallow hard like I'm taking a pill,
have to push my forehead closer to
what I know is cold wind rushing outside the window,
to stop myself from saying,

Jesus. Me too.

When my brother says the name of the band,
you don't commit it to memory the way other people would:
Typing what they don't want to forget into their phones.
Writing on the backs of their hands.
Repeating it silently to themselves
until they know all the words by heart.

No.
You trace the letters up the length of my arm
as if I am an extension of you.
Then you stare into my eyes, hard and long,
demanding, without words, that I remember too.

This is another part of our
thousand-pronged problem:
there are moments when our heads
and hearts
and bodies

align so exactly that I know losing you
would unravel the fabric of my universe.

But in the same second,
the same breath,
I am hit with another truth:
having you any more completely
than I already do
might bring the same ruinous reckoning.

*   *   *

The roads are a little icy since it's so cold
and my brother drives more carefully than he normally would.
And it's endless, this road,
this feeling.
This closeness that is too close
but not nearly close enough.

Just before your exit,
you slip your gloves on and put your warm hand on my knee.
The fabric is soft when I cover your hidden fingers
with my own, which are ashy from the cold,
weathered and exposed.

You say, *Worth it?*
Because you never regret anything
and I perpetually do.

I nod even though it's not what I mean.
It's not even close to being true.

You believe me,
because you only ever say what you mean.
That, or nothing at all.
You can't imagine truth as anything
but a window.
But for me it's a collapsing brick wall.

So I lie. And you smile.
And I look at our hands again, wondering
how we can touch so gently when we're so monstrously in love,
how there can be so much peace between two chaotic neutrals like
    us,
how storm-swollen feelings can fit into our tiny human hearts,
and how part of me doesn't regret it.
Part of me was maybe telling some version of the truth.
The part of me that can't think of anyone
I'd rather burn down the world with
than you.

373 DAYS BEFORE THE FIRE

Last year, you looked at me and out of nowhere you said:

There's a chemical reason
  pouring water over a fire
    puts it out.

Just like there's a chemical reason I want to be
          on top
            of you.

We both laughed hard.
But then you didn't speak to me for three days.

I learned you run when things get too real.
When you think and feel and say too much.
I learned to tiptoe around the truth of us
as if it were a sleeping dog
I didn't want to wake.

We haven't been the same since.

We will never be the same again.

8. We're both monsters

I've tried to explain
us
to my brother more times than I can count.

It's not like we live in some Podunk town, he says
as soon as you drop out of the truck.
He noticed our hands I guess, or maybe all the invisible ways
we are always touching.
It's not like anyone would care.

It's not about anyone else, I say for the millionth time.
It's about us.

I don't get it, he says again before he turns up the radio.
I glare at him and turn it back down.

My shoulders tense up when he says this
because he's one of the very few humans
who gets just about every piece of me.

So I stay quiet.
I think hard.
I try one more time.

It's like that book, I start.
The one with the kid and the monsters.
The forest in his room

and the boat
and the still-hot soup?

Okay . . . he says.
But I can tell by his voice that he's with me.
I sit up farther in my seat.

It's like that part where the monsters tell him
I'll eat you up, I love you so,
and the kid screams no?

I think I'm following you.

We're both monsters, I say.
Me and her.

She is moody and
bizarrely kind and
gorgeous and
intense.

She needs very little, but what she needs she cannot go without.

I'm reckless and
oddly sweet and
gentle and
possessive.

I want what I want when I want it and fast.
I'm a collector of rare and beautiful things
and she is the rarest and most beautiful of all.

But I can't stomach failing to meet her every need.
And she will not be owned.

And yet:
We each want to eat the other up.
There's no one to scream no.
No one to stop us from
devouring each other.

If we were anything more
than whatever the hell we already are,
there would be no survivors, I tell him.
Do you understand?

He nods slowly and grips the wheel tighter.
I look out the window again and my chest aches
from the gorgeous, sad music
and the unveiled truth of these words.

There wouldn't be anyone left.

349 DAYS BEFORE THE FIRE

I went to my granny's house
when I realized what was happening.
When I realized that I loved you
and you might love me back.

I burst through her green front door,
sighing and sobbing and saying,
Why the hell can't I just be her friend?

She sat me at her table
and put the kettle on
and slipped a thick slice of pound cake
onto a saucer right in front of me.

Baby, she said.
You know I'm an old lady.
You have to tell me everything
start to finish
before we can start or finish anything else.

So I cried and I ate and talked,
and she watched me through her big, smudged glasses.
I stared at her pearly white hair,
her thin, rough fingers,
remembering.

When I was younger
she would press my hair for special occasions.
Slather it with grease as green as her front door
before Easter or a wedding or a funeral.
And as I learned to trust her steady hands
with that smoking hot comb,
I learned I could trust her with my secrets, too.

She is the one who taught me that
love is in the listening.

When I'd finished the cake and the story,
she sat back.
She said, *Umhm.*
She slapped her knees
and licked her lips
and stood up.

She walked to the fridge
and took out everything she needed
to make (my favorite) buttermilk biscuits.
Without a word she started to work,
then looked back at me
like I was a lazy cat
or a dumb dog.

Her eyes were on fire
behind her big granny glasses.
She said: *Get over here, girl.*
And I flew to her side.

The thing about biscuit dough, she said,
is that you gotta show it love.
Be gentle, go slow, and remember:
everything you're doing is to help it rise.

We mixed the flour and butter,
salt and sugar and milk.
Then she let me knead the dough.
My hands felt too small,
too hesitant,
for such important work,
but Gran's hands soon covered mine like a blanket:
two dark, wrinkly guides.

See? she said as it started to come together.
All you have to do is take your time.
And I thought I got what she meant:
that every little thing about me
and everything about you
would eventually mix and mingle
into something smooth and new.

But she didn't answer my question.
So with flour-dusted fingers, I asked it again.

Why can't we just be friends?

I don't know, boo, she said.
Some people just ain't meant to be.
She went back to the dough.
That was all she had to say.

(In the moment, I thought she meant
we weren't meant to be friends.
But now I wonder if she knew before I did:
that you were you and I was me
and we weren't meant to be
anything.)

We cut out biscuits with
Gran's biscuit-cutting cup
and baked them till they were crown high,
swollen, and golden.

I cried again looking at them
because they were so beautiful.
Brown and thick and warm
just like you.

*   *   *

Later, I said I was sorry for all the weeping.
For yelling and storming in and making a scene.
And Gran just kissed my forehead and shrugged
while pushing cloth-wrapped, still-warm biscuits
into my hands.

You can be as blue as you wanna be, she said.
Because I know you're gold inside.

I felt my tears well again.

You're the bluest girl I know
but also the goldest.

But Gran, I said,
I still don't know what to do.

Less doing, baby.
More being.

And if you must do something,
just show her love.
Be gentle, go slow, only help her rise.
By the time it's time to do something else,
my blue, golden girl,
you'll know.

9. This could get ugly

When me and my brother get home,
I'm shook as I walk through the back door.

My parents are there, lying in wait.
They could be jaguars,
or a pair of creepy old paintings:
still and silent and scary,
with haunted, haunting eyes.
And just like a big cat,
just like antique art,
I know I'll get in trouble
if I get too close.

I thought
since my brother had answered the phone,
had picked us up,
had saved us,
that I'd be safe for a few more hours
from this inevitable parental rage.
But here they are,
sitting at the breakfast table,
phone in front of their folded hands.

My dad says:
The school called back.
My mom says:
Your brother's good but he ain't that good.

I say (in my head):
Shit.

My brother slinks past and salutes me,
his hand striking the air in front of his brow.
Says, *Nice knowing you, kid,*
and skips up to his room.

I guess because it was so early
when we got into trouble
they hadn't even left for work yet.
So they're here and I'm here and this could get ugly.

My father enjoys quoting the Bible, but my mama,
she likes quoting famous women.
And I'd take her gospel over his
any day of the week.

The real problem is:
he likes to think God's wrath is scary to me.
But he couldn't be more wrong.
A peaceful heavenly father isn't nearly as threatening as
a pissed-off earthly mother.
Not when I was little,
not now,
and probably not ever.

So after Daddy tells me all the biblical reasons
what I did was wrong —

Thou shalt honor your mother and father.
Thou shalt not steal (I guess he means the newspapers).
Do unto others as you would have them do unto you.
And one I hadn't heard before:
Scoffers set a city aflame, but the wise turn away wrath.
— instead of just telling me what *he* thinks,
I say, *'Kay, sorry, Daddy,* and turn, with mounting nerves,
to face Mama.

She slides a steaming cup of warm, dark tea
sweetened with honey
into my hands,
and for too long a time, she doesn't say anything.
I'm terrified to speak first.
So I just sit there, sipping and sweating.

A woman is like a tea bag, Mama finally says,
slowly stirring her own drink
like a villain twirling a mustache.
She looks up at me, her eyes dark
and as fierce as Gran's get sometimes.
You never know how strong she is until
she gets in hot water.

Eleanor Roosevelt, right? I ask quickly,
hoping I'll score some points for knowing.
Yeah, and nice try, she says,
but trivia won't save your tail this time.

She calls me by all three of my names
and says she can't believe I would do something so stupid.
You're a smart girl, she says,
too smart for something as dumb as this.
What in the world were you thinking?

And this is the only reason I sometimes prefer
my father's methods
to my mother's.
His scriptures don't require anything of me.
They don't leave room for my words,
my thoughts,
my feelings.

He doesn't ask me how or why or what.
Maybe because he doesn't want to know.

Maybe he wouldn't know what to do with the truth:
That I hurt in huge, unstoppable ways
(that he can't fix).
That there are things burning inside me that can only be
        extinguished
by setting something else on fire.
That chaos is normal
and confusion is natural
and everything is more out of control than he thinks.

(Especially me.)

But Mama? She's a detective.
She needs to know everything
and she won't stop asking until
she has all the info she craves.

This is why she knows me more than he ever will:
She asks. She waits. And when I speak,
just like Gran,
she listens.

So I tell her about the swimsuit.
About the gym teacher.
About the guy calling you a cow.
About homework and headaches
and heartaches and you.
I felt powerless, I say.
I felt like no one was paying attention.
I felt like no one cared that
everything was terrible.
I tell her that so many things were on fire already,
so what was a dumpster?
What was one more thing that might hurt later
if it made me feel seen and strong
and a tiny bit powerful now?

I get it, she says.
You know you still wrong as hell,
but I get it.

Slowly, I grin.
I know I'm still in trouble, but there's something sacred
about a parent saying
those three words.

I get it, she says.
And I go from feeling invisible
to feeling like I fill the whole room,
the whole building,
the whole sky.

Only two people have ever made me feel that seen:
my mother
and you.

Her understanding settles around my shoulders like a blanket.
Like something bigger and better than love.

She goes to the stove.
Lifts the kettle.
Adds more hot water to both our cups.
Because we are women.
And we are like tea bags.
And we have enough strength left in us
to make two whole new cups
of tea.

A truth:

Our love was never gentle.
Never slow.
Never rising.

So I couldn't take my time,
the way Gran said,
as much as I wanted to.

Everything about us was
too hard and quick,
and we were always
falling fast.

I didn't know how to stop it.

322 DAYS BEFORE THE FIRE

Your empty house haunted us both.

Where is everyone? I asked
for maybe the fiftieth time.

(Shadows as tall as me painted the walls.)

Not here, you answered, the way you always did.

(Your voice almost echoed.)

And usually that was it. Usually, I let it go.
But when you called me,
I could tell that you'd been crying.
And I was angry you were always so alone.
I wanted to know why there was never
anyone but me
loving you.

(Our footsteps were an earthquake.)

No, but really, I said.
Your mom? Your dad? Your sister?
Why are they never home?

You leaned against a blank wall in the hall.
Recounted your family's whereabouts,
counting each person with your fingers.

(And your sigh was as loud as the wind in this kind of quiet.)

Dad's traveling for work, like always.
Mom is across town volunteering
or protesting
or organizing . . .
She's very dedicated to "the cause."

      Which cause?

All of them.

      And your sister?

She's always at her boyfriend's place.

There, in that blank bit of hallway,
I could feel a void inside you
that wasn't too unlike the one inside me.

I hugged you then,
like I was the exact shape
of the hole in you.

You squeezed me back,
like you would fit perfectly into mine.

* * *

In the basement,
we swapped secrets.

I lined up my grandfather's whiskey stones on your pillow
and told you I'd named them
John, Paul, George, and Ringo.

You showed me how you'd stacked your books
so that the spines in each pile made a poem.

I helped you untangle your hair.

You gently touched my birthmark —
a pale blotch of skin shaped like Russia in an ocean of brown
on my thigh —
and I laced my fingers through yours when I couldn't take it
      anymore.

I painted your nails and you painted gloss across my lips
and we danced until we were sweaty.
We lay down, side by side, to try to cool off.

You went quiet.
And (though you knew me better than anyone)
there was still this part of you
that felt infinitely unknowable.

I wanted to look at you,
to touch you,
to *know* you,
but I just closed my eyes.

You fill me up, you know that? you said.
And it was so much,
that tiny piece of truth.
You were always so alone.
We needed each other so desperately.
My heart felt swollen.
I didn't know what to say back.

So I opened my eyes.
Looked at you slow and close.
And blanketed your body
with mine
until you laughed.

* * *

I knew how to love in a way that made your house
and you
feel less abandoned.
And you loved me in a way
that meant I carried fewer things around in my pockets.

For years I'd felt like I was disappearing.
And the treasures and trinkets I held close
helped me feel like I was really

Here.

But you made me know it.
That I was here.
That my hereness was important.
No.
That my hereness was *essential*.
That if I faded away, there would be someone
other than my family
who noticed.

And how do you say thank you for that?

(How do I ever stop saying
thank you
for something like that?)

10. Spilled ink

I text you the second I get to my room.
What did your parents say?

If we were at school, we'd be texting from our separate classes,
so in a way, it feels completely natural.
Like a normal Monday morning where we didn't
start a fire.

They're not home, you send back.

Mine are, I type.
Then I delete the message without sending it.

This is something we don't really talk about:
The ubiquity of my parents.
The absence of yours.
The extent to which they influence
our lives
and our heads
and our hearts
when it comes to how we deal
with the harshness of reality and love.

You know my parents are going to call yours, I type,
and then I delete that, too.

Talking is so much easier than texting.
Especially with you.
But when I tell you that, you don't listen.
You laugh.

What are you going to do for the rest of the day? I send instead.
Because I could imagine you lying there,
reading in (y)our basement
or flicking your lighter open and shut,
curls like spilled ink or spilled secrets,
legs like dark puddles or the darkest clouds,
in your bed
on your own,
dreaming of flames and fury.

Music turned up so high it hurts
because the silence of your house
was always too loud for you to take.

Dunno, you answer.

Do something with me, I type, then erase.
Let's do something together, I type, then erase.
I want to do something with you, I type, then erase.

Dammit, I say.

I don't want to be alone, I think,
full of angst and agony,
but don't even lift my thumbs to the screen.

And then,
in one of our synced mental moments,
the ones I both love and hate,
you send:
I don't want to be alone
so I don't have to be the one who needs something.
So I can be the hero this time.

You're always in my head
and I want you there
as desperately as I don't.

Maybe this is why you like texting.
Because there's a secret to me that not many people know.
But maybe you do:

Writing makes me share things that are much closer to the truth.

I'm coming over, I reply right away.

You text back in an instant:

Hurry.

316 DAYS BEFORE THE FIRE

The first time we slept together
I thought I wouldn't survive it.

It was my sixteenth birthday
and you'd been promising me a surprise for weeks.

I told you all I wanted
was to hang out in (y)our basement.
That I didn't need any gifts from anyone,
especially not you.

But you didn't listen.
And you gave me the worst,
best gift of all time:

you gave me
even more
of you.

Your front door flew open
before I even knocked.
And your hands flew to my face
before I even saw them coming.
Shhh, you said, covering my eyes.

Okay, I whispered.
But why do I have to be quiet?

Shhhh, you said again, louder.
You just do.

In a few quick steps,
we were at the basement stairs,
so you uncovered my eyes.
But it was so dark I could barely see
more than a few feet in front of me.

The whole house was as silent as a library.
As silent as sleeping.
As silent as I am when I have to go to church.
Nobody's home, right? I asked.
You shook your head.

I should have known
what was coming.

You made me walk down the stairway backwards,
and you kept the lights off, so I still couldn't see.
I'm going to break my ass, I said.
You won't. I've got you, you promised me.

We were careful.
I stepped gingerly and you held my hands.
I knew the stairs by heart.
I couldn't make out much of you
through the thick, deep dark,
but I stared anyway.

I landed at the bottom and then
looked up at where you stood
a step behind me.
A step above me.

We have always been precisely
the same height,
but when I dreamt of you,
you were always taller
like this.
In that moment,
with you on the higher step,
you were the you from my imagination.
Literally larger than you were in real life.

Hey, you said.
Oh hey, I said.
You grinned and stepped down and then behind me.
And though my eyes followed your face
like a lighthouse,
you wouldn't let me turn all the way around.

Your fingers were there again,
smelling sweet and smoky,
feeling warm and tender,
covering my eyes.
My hands floated up to clasp your wrists like
twin bracelets,
and slowly, we both spun around.

Happy birthday, you said,
and as your hands slid from my eyes
to my shoulders,
I saw my surprise.

The basement was always full of candles
but now they were lit.
Tiny golden beacons were
in every corner,
on every surface,
along every wall.

Oh my God, I said, laughing.
What the hell is this?

And as we stepped out of the shadows
and into the room's gilded glow,
I could finally see you fully.

Your eyes were lined and your lids glittered.
Your cheeks were pinked and your lips shimmered.
The dress you were wearing
and your nails were both my favorite color:
a dark ocean blue.
And your hair was everywhere.

I swallowed hard and asked more slowly,
Wait. What's going on?

I'm ... your surprise, you said.

And then, before I could blink,
you stepped so close to me
that I stopped breathing.

I said your name.
You said mine.
We said we wouldn't, I whispered.
You said, *I changed my mind.*

Do you not want to? you asked,
and your eyes looked wet.
We don't have to if you don't want to.
I just thought ...

You know I want to.

And almost instantly
I was
drowning.

We were
a sea storm:
wet and wind-tossed and wild.
Desperate and deliberate and dependent
on only each other.

(And I was gasping.)

Are you okay?
God, yes.

We were
a brush fire:
hot and harrowing and hungry.
Excited and exploding and expanding
into new versions of ourselves.

(And you were roaring and raging.)

Do you want me to stop?
Never.

We were
a crossword puzzle.
You were full of incomplete clues,
but I knew all the answers
to every empty space inside you.

Can I?
Do it.

Down and across we went,
filling in every blank that ever existed
between us.
And we may have screamed every four-letter word we knew,
but the only one that mattered was

l o v e.

Your hands were full of my hips.
My hands were full of your hair.
And my body shook with the knowledge
of how long and how badly I'd wanted you.

We were
knuckles and knees,
shoulders and shins,
elbows and toes,
fingertips and lips.

I kissed every inch of you.
And you stroked every inch of me.
And we each
discovered
every centimeter
of the other.

But I suspected, even as it ended,
even as we cuddled and cackled,
whimpered and wept,
that because I was still me
and you were still you,

everything
and nothing
had changed.

A lie:

"Friends with benefits."

The truth?
Friends with deficits.

11. Lock and key

The second my parents leave for work,
I drive to your house.

I am breaking every rule there is to break
but they'll never know.
My brother's not a snitch,
and thank God for that
because after I pull a wool hat over my nearly bald head,
I yell up to him that I'm taking his truck.

This,
you and me,
cannot wait.

As I drive, I try not to think
about what we've done,
about what we've become.
But I can feel your loneliness in my chest
and it's like asthma:
heavy and taut and impossible to escape.

I know there are moments when
you feel my misery too:
It's a tiny fist just behind my sternum, you told me once.
A knot just above my heart,
a spring coiled right below my clavicle,
squeezed tight and aching.

I pull out my phone at a stoplight
to send: *I'm close*
before I actually am.
I have to tell you now
so the door will be open when I get there.
And I need to get there as quickly as I can.

No you aren't, you send back.
And I can imagine you smiling down at my lie.
But I know you're walking upstairs too,
just in case this is one of the few times
you should believe me.

I don't think about the empty gaps inside me
that you fill.
I don't think about my sorrow taking up the space
you need to breathe.
I stare at the only road that leads to you
and I don't stop going
straight and fast
until I get there.

*　*　*

When I pull up
your door is unlocked like I wanted.
I ease inside and stomp downstairs.

Hey, you say.

You've rested your head on the arm of one of your sofas
(no need for a pillow, thanks to your billowing hair),
a book, like always, in your soft brown hands.

Oh hey, I say, closing the distance between us.

It's barely been an hour,
but I jump onto the couch
and kiss you
like we haven't seen each other in weeks.

Then I curl around you,
wet lips against dry neck,
soft belly to firm back,
thighs on thighs,
knees tucked inside knees,
and sigh.

We only fit on the sofa together
because we fit together:
Like puzzle pieces.
Like a lock and key.
Like we were manufactured,
made and molded,
to lie clutching each other
this way.

I haven't been sleeping, you whisper.
I keep having these dreams.
Sleep now, I say into your hair.
I'll chase the bad away.

You do.
You drop into sleep like you've fallen off a cliff:
steeply, suddenly, deeply.
And as I feel your breathing slow,
your body relaxing against mine,
your head getting heavier and all its racing thoughts easing to a
    crawl,
whatever part of you
that was holding my chest hostage
loosens its grip.

I breathe you in.
That something sweet I'm used to
tinged with smoke.
And as I breathe out
I can almost forget that we're in trouble,
that I'm breaking even more rules right now.
That school is unbearable,
and life isn't fair,
and you are unpredictable,
and we're completely out of control.

Because you are in my hands.

And you are breathing, slow and steady.

And you are trusting me to guard you.

(And I will guard you with my life.)

I will keep the bad away so you can get some rest.

Fight all your demons, even the ones I cannot see.

And right now,

this couch that holds you and me —

the weight of our feelings and fears,

of our dreams

and our bodies —

is the entire universe.

As far as I'm concerned,

nothing else matters.

Nothing else even exists.

299 DAYS BEFORE THE FIRE

When it was your sixteenth birthday,
just a few weeks after mine,
I didn't know what to do.
I'd bought you something months earlier,
but now it didn't seem like enough.

What could I possibly give you
that would be as gentle or as beautiful
as how we'd held each other
in the dark?

I'd spent days thinking,
always coming up empty,
until that day,
in my car,
when I was already halfway to your house.

I'd thought of this idea before and decided against it
(and if I was being honest, I thought about it all the time),
but I also thought that maybe things might be different now
with you or me or us,
especially after . . . everything.

* * *

We'd planned to watch trailers in your basement.
It was one of our things.

Trailers over everything, I'd always say.
Because the promise of something is better than the actual thing,
you'd reply.
Almost always,
we'd finish together.

So the lights were out.
Candles were lit.
And we were projecting the trailers onto the ceiling
from where we were lying on the floor.

We'd piled soft blankets and pillows
over the rainbow
and your head was on my belly.
My fingers were in your hair.

We were watching trailers of all our favorite '80s movies:
The Breakfast Club
and *The Outsiders.*
Dirty Dancing
and *Dead Poets Society.*

We ignored how there were no brown faces to be found
and focused only on how good the music was.
How the teens in these movies were
mad and messy mavericks,
so moody and so much
like us.

I had it all planned out.
I'd made the playlist.
Queued the trailers up in an order
that flowed like the best movie soundtrack.
It would end with *Sixteen Candles,*
and I'd baked you a rainbow cake.

So we cuddled and commented,
watched and whispered,
and right before we reached the final trailer,
I grabbed your cake from the kitchen
and lit the sixteen candles on top.
You grinned as I came down the stairs, singing.

Make a wish, I said, so you closed your pretty eyes
and then made the flames disappear, like magic.

I handed you your gifts.
You ripped them open.
A slim book of poetry in one hand.
A small silver lighter in the palm of the other.
A rose was on the book's cover,
and another was carved into one side of the lighter.
Both were inscribed, too.
But you hadn't even flipped the book open
or the lighter over to see
before you hug-tackled me.

The inside of the book's cover said:
Words to keep you company whenever I can't.
And the back of the lighter read:
"These violent delights have violent ends,"
a part of your favorite line from *Romeo + Juliet.*
(*The Baz Luhrmann movie,*
you'd be quick to tell anyone without shame,
not the play.)

You paged through the book.
Read a line or two to me, whispering.
Flicked the lighter open and sparked a flame.
Used your thumb to slam it shut.
You glanced up at me, grinning.

They're perfect, you said.

A second later, I looked right at you,
and though my mouth felt desert-dry,
I swallowed hard
and asked,

Will you be my girlfriend?

The pause was long and empty.
Then your face changed so fast it was like
you'd pulled a mask on.

Why would you ask me that? you said.
And half a million reasons ran through my head:

Because your brain is as beautiful as your hair.
Because you'd fight anyone and anything for me.
Because your hand fits perfectly inside mine.
Because if you need me, I'll come for you from anywhere at any
     time.
Because I always want to know how you're sleeping.
Because I always want to know what you're thinking.
Because I can feel you in my chest.
Because you smell of sweet smoke and you listen to every word I
     say.
Because I have never felt like this before. Ever.

Because
we're
us.

But what I said was:
Because I like you.

I blinked
one,
two,
three times,
into the silence.

Because I . . . more than like you.

(A submarine of an understatement. A quick, quiet lie.)

We already talked about this,
you said, moving away from me.
And we said we wouldn't.

It was exactly what I'd said two weeks ago,
on *my* birthday,
almost in this exact spot,
moments before we stood naked in front of each other
for the first fragile time.

I repeated what you said to me then:
I changed my mind.

But before I could smirk,
before I could grab your elbow or your belt loop
and pull you back close to me again,
you frowned and said:

Well, you don't get to.

You looked up at the ceiling,
where Molly Ringwald was frozen,
sitting in front of her crush, in front of her cake,
in a frilly pink dress neither of us would ever wear.

You punched me with your eyes and said:
The promise of something is better than the actual thing, remember?

Almost always, I'd said not so long ago.

But not always.
Not now,
with us.

I felt the weight of a skeleton key in my pocket.

Slipped my fingers around it to make sure I was still real.
I'd brought it for bravery, but
I was caught in the riptide of your rejection,
and no matter how tightly I gripped it,
I couldn't say anything.

It's too much, you said next.
And this was not going how I'd imagined it would.

My face must have asked the question, *What is?*
Because, though my mouth was still frozen, you answered.

You. Us. This.
It's suffocating.

How is it suffocating? my eyes must have questioned.

Do I really have to say it? you asked me.
And I found my voice.

I said *yes* because I didn't understand.

You're always here, you said.

Where else am I supposed to be?

Your eyes filled so fast I almost didn't notice.
But then
I did.

I'd never seen you cry
and I got so scared
that I froze again.
But we're opposites.
When you're terrified,
you run.

Your eyes were shining as you grabbed
your wallet, and keys, and phone.
We were in your house, but you packed your bag
as if we were in mine.

God. You're impossible, you said.
And I just sat, staring.

I couldn't move,
like someone had pressed pause on me, too,
and not just the movie trailer on the ceiling.

Where are you going? I asked. *Why would you leave?*

You threw your bag over your shoulder.
Shoved your feet, hard, into your shoes.

At the bottom of the stairs, you looked back at me
just for a second
before running up them,
like I was dangerous.
Like the basement was on fire.

From the top, I heard your loud, clear voice,
just before the front door slammed.

You screamed:

> *I love you so much I can't fucking breathe.*

And then,
like the flames on your birthday candles,
you were gone.

12. Menu of Possibility

When you wake up,
we stare at the ceiling,
at the stars and planets that make a flat, fathomable universe
above our heads,
and we realize today might be our last day of freedom
for a while.

Suspensions and sneaking out and setting fires
are not reasons our parents should trust us,
and we may not see each other
after today
for weeks.

So
we go to the bridge.

It's right at the edge of town,
long and spindly like a giant spider.
Metal and fire-engine red,
like it should have its own siren.

It's single-laned and slippery when wet.
Only one car can cross at a time.
And it sits above a river that separates
our town from the one next to it.

The bridge tells people from either side
(us or them)
to slow down.
To take turns.
Exactly how and when it's okay to enter
somewhere that is not home.

We love that it's an in-between place.
A not-quite-here, not-quite-there space.
There are only so many ways to experience your
bigness and smallness at once,
you said to me the first time we came here.
And we stood still right in the center of it for a long time,
staring at the sky,
feeling insignificant and infinite,
impossibly in two places
at once.

Now
coins dot the river's banks and bottom,
making everything shine and glint
in the midmorning sun.
And we lean over, counting up change
that people threw away like they could
pay for things to be different.

Everyone comes here
to sit with their legs suspended above the water.
To toss pennies

like flickering fireflies
over the edge.
But because we're us,
we, of course, have slightly different plans.

We add to the Menu of Possibility:
A list we began scratching into the bridge's metal posts
when we were fifteen.
Prices we gave to certain wishes.

$0.20 for good grades.
$0.35 to make the team.
$0.75 for parents who understand.

$1.85 for a great first kiss.
$2.60 to graduate, no matter what.
$5.00 flat to get the hell out of here.

What should we charge to forget? I ask you.

Forget what?

Anything. Everything.

Why do you want to forget everything? you ask.

So I can be fresh. New.
Unruined in all the ways that I am.

You're not ruined. Or if you are, so am I.

    So is everyone.

Exactly. Ruined is normal, you say.
Broken is average. Messy is more than okay.
Imperfect is perfect, because we're all pretty fucked up.

I smile.
Push your wild hair away from your wild eyes.
I want to kiss you, but I don't.

You reach up like you're going to touch my cheek,
but you lay your gloved hand right in the center of my chest.
I breathe deep, feeling a little less
ruined and broken, messy and imperfect.
You smile back.

    So . . . free? I ask, pulling out my car key.

Maybe like five cents.

    Cool, I say.

And remembering should cost more.

I scratch it all into the metal,
the prices we assigned to
keeping or losing our memories.

You sit on the cold wrought iron
and let your legs hang down,
bootlaces dangling.
You pull out your lighter.
Flick it open and shut,
open and shut.

Into the water,
we toss stones instead of coins.
We talk about our dreams
instead of making wishes.
And when you get bored
and I get hungry,
we add one more thing to the bridge menu
before we get up and go.

To never doubt that someone loves you;
to just know when it is so.

We can't agree on a price.

281 DAYS BEFORE THE FIRE

A boy asked you out.
You told me you were thinking about it.
Even after everything
that had happened on our birthdays.
(Maybe because of everything
that had happened on our birthdays?)

The thought of you holding his hand
instead of mine
tore something open inside me.

I was not okay.

Why him? I demanded.
What's so special about him?
What I really meant was
Why not me?
(But I'm a liar, and a coward, so that is not what I said.)

I don't know, you said.
Your eyes flicked to him.
He's cute.

My eyes followed yours and found him
where he sat on the other side of the cafeteria.
He had toffee-brown skin

and black, bushy hair.
Dimples and glasses and a wicked-looking grin.
Is he? I asked.

(I'd liked boys before, but their faces were always harder for me to
     navigate.
They were maps of foreign countries
with cities and towns listed in languages I couldn't always
     understand.
But girls' faces were novels written in my native tongue.
Girls' faces were poetry.)

You shrugged. Looked back down.
He's nice.

I thought about him handing you a homework packet.
About him laughing at something you said.
About his deep, thunderstorm voice
booming down the hallway in your direction, saying:
What's the story, morning glory?
(You loved that.)
Is he? I asked.

(I'd liked boys before, but their kindness was lost on me.
It always felt conditional, sullied, strained.
And when they were angry, their meanness was swift and
     dangerous.
Girls could be mean too, of course, and they could do even more
     damage.

But their kindness landed as lightly as butterfly wings.
Their "nice" was rarely laced with ice.)

Oh my God, you said.
Why are you freaking out?
I just kinda have a crush on him, okay?
It's not a big deal.

Your cheek was so recently pressed against my hip in the dark.
We'd held hands the night before while we were sleeping in the
    same bed.
You'd cried with your head on my shoulder that morning.

(I'd liked boys before, but I'd never loved anyone like I loved you.)

You were mine.
            But you weren't mine.

                      My insides were being ripped apart.

It's not? I asked.

A lie:

"Sweet sixteen."

The truth?
Sixteen isn't sweet.
Or maybe it's so sweet it makes you sick.
Makes you ache.

Whoever came up with that phrase must have forgotten
what it's like to be a teenager.
What it's like to feel foreign in your own family,
your own head,
your own body,
your own life.

Or maybe it was made up by someone
who had never been a kid
at all.

13. Her pt. 1

Going to the movies is your idea.

I don't want to risk it.
I say, *If you want to watch something,*
let's do it in the basement,
sprawled across your floor,
with a million lit candles,
staring at the ceiling.

It's free.
We can touch as little or as much as we want.
And we don't have to worry about being seen,
or worse: picked up for truancy.

But you aren't into it.

I want to see something new, you say.
I want surround sound and a big, bright screen.
I want to eat buttery popcorn
and kiss you in the dark.

Fine, I say.
Because I always let you have your way.

I buy the tickets and you handle the snacks.
Chocolate-covered raisins
and a bucket of popcorn.

Smothered nachos
and beer you brought from home,
smuggled in under your puffy coat.

We pick a weird indie movie
that will probably make no sense.
But it stars gorgeous people in pretty places,
surrounded by bokeh and just the right amount of lens flare,
and maybe, hopefully,
water sparkling behind them —
every shot, a dream.

There will be witty banter
and slow-motion drives
and a killer soundtrack:
the only things we care about.

We make out during the opening credits.
You taste like salty chocolate and cheap, bitter beer;
like being a little kid and being all grown up
at once.

As the movie starts,
you do this thing
where you cup the back of my head
like it's a goblet,
or something else as delicate as glass.
It drove me wild before, when I had hair,
but now, with barely any left,

I can feel every one of your thin fingers,
the pleasant rake of your nails,
the soft skin of your palm.
It makes me shiver.

Are you cold? you ask in a whisper.
I shake my head.
Pull away quick to avoid your questions.
To avoid telling a truth that might send you running.

I take a sip of beer.
Then stare at the screen so I won't stare at you.

We watch for a while.
It stars a white girl with wispy blond hair,
a white guy with a golden goatee.
He has a redheaded sister and slightly brown friends.
She has a skinny freckled kid brother
who says funny things
right when the dramatic tension is highest.

It's about love,
because almost every story is,
and they have simple problems like:
Wondering if the other person loves them back.
Wondering if they should take the new job in a new city.
Wondering if their best friend is mad at them.
Wondering why their life is so confusing.

I wish those were the things I had to worry about.

I know you love me back. (It doesn't change anything.)
I know I'm stuck right where I am. (Just trying to make it through
    high school.)
I know you're always mad at me. (Even when I don't know why.)
And then when you aren't, I know that you will be again too soon.

I know exactly why my life is so confusing.

But maybe that's the point of the movie.
That even when you're beautiful
and white
and rich
and your life is full of a million choices,
shit is still hard.

Movies like this forget
or maybe ignore
or maybe don't even think about
how their beauty and whiteness and richness
isn't a part of what makes their lives difficult.
And how shit's even more impossible
for people like us.

About halfway through the movie,
you cup the back of my head again
and I tremble, because I can't help it.

Take my sweater, you say.
You slip out of your hoodie,
shove it into my lap.
It's not that, I tell you,
but a chorus of *Shhhhhh*s
reminds me I'm no good at whispering.

You're the one who's always cold,
not me.
And right away I see goose bumps
creeping up your arm.
But you gave me your sweater
and it smells like you.
So I slip my arms in,
sink into it like warm water.

I never finish saying what I wanted:
It's not that,
you gorgeous girl.
It's you.

* * *

After the movie, we're in the hallway
waiting for the line to the bathroom to die down.
You sit on the cushy carpet
and I hop around you in a circle,
pointing at the movie posters,
asking if you want to see

this or
this or
what about that?

When we finally get into the white-walled restroom,
we pee, then splash water on each other at the sinks.
And while we're yell-singing over the too-loud whir of the hand
    dryers,
feeling free and fearless,

we bump into
her.

274 DAYS BEFORE THE FIRE

I went out with a girl from church.
Only because you were out with that boy.
She went to a private school
and I liked that no one knew her.
She was pretty and sweet and she invited me to a party.

She told me to meet her at the end of a dirt road
that looked like it led to nowhere.
And since I couldn't drive yet,
I begged my brother to drop me off.

This looks sketchy AF, he said.
I don't know if I want to leave you here.

But then she appeared,
looking innocent and adorable,
and he must have figured I could handle it.
A breezy girl like her
probably seemed harmless
when he was so used to me
hanging out with a whirlwind
like you.

Hey, I said.
I let her hold my hand as I hopped out of the truck.
Hey yourself, she said back.

When I reached for it, she let me touch her hair:
long thin braids with shells on the ends.
I tucked one behind her ear.

She was nothing like you.
Her smile was sweet and dimpled.
Her dress knee-length with pockets.
Her voice was soft but her laugh sounded evil.
I kind of liked her right away.

My curfew is midnight, I said
as my brother drove off.
That cool?

It's whatever, she said.
She pointed toward a dense crop of trees.
We're going in there.

Through the tree line were five big mansions,
all set back a safe distance from the freeway.
The party was here, at a fancy, abandoned subdivision:
houses half-finished, roads half-paved.

All the markers of safety
normally in a place like this
were missing:
The wholesome yellow signs.
The neighborhood watch.
The speed bumps.

The cul-de-sac.
The even, too-green lawns.

It was a ghost town,
and I kind of liked that it was incomplete and imperfect.
My heart fluttered because it felt a little dangerous —
the opposite of what they'd intended it to be.

I think the developer got tied up in some weird lawsuit,
she said as we crept closer.
Ran out of money or something
and killed the construction contract
before they were done.

I spotted a weathered sign that said TEMPLE HEIGHTS,
and I read it out loud.
Yeah, she said. *But we call it the Sub.*

*   *   *

I could hear music as we got closer,
and when we walked into the first big house,
it was packed with white kids.

They were dancing and smoking and drinking,
kissing and laughing and shouting,
lighting firecrackers on the dusty floor
and kicking holes in the already crumbling walls.

It was just the kind of chaos you would have loved.
I looked around and smirked.

Want a drink? she asked,
leading me forward by the hand.
Obviously, I said.
Even though the only person I'd ever gotten drunk with
was you.

As I sipped and she flirted,
I couldn't figure out how to relax.
She and I were the only two Black kids there,
and I couldn't stop imagining
a police raid where we were the only victims.
So even as everyone around us raged,
we whispered.

My gran says places like this have a certain energy
and you have to be careful not to disturb the peace.
She nodded like I'd just said the best shit ever,
and pulled a pack of tarot cards out of her pocket.

I knew the reading would be about you
before she even laid the cards in front of me.
And when the Empress showed up, upside down between
the Three of Cups and the Ten of Wands,
I knew I'd been right.

The little I'd learned about tarot was thanks to Gran,
who was witchy in the way
most old Black ladies are churchy.
Her milky eyes and gnarled fingers and wild, white curls
were the kinds of features fortune-tellers have in books.
Her face alone was usually enough for people to believe
every word she said.

Now my date,
who had somehow become my seer,
shook her braids out of her eyes.
She looked at the cards,
looked at me,
then looked back at the cards again.

This card, she said, touching the one on my left
with only her fingertips,
is your past.
The Three of Cups represents platonic love,
maybe someone who is a close and loving friend.

This one, she said, touching the card
in the center,
is the now.
The Empress is reversed,
so she is giving you a warning.
There is a presence in your life that may be hurting you
whether you want to admit it
or not.

And this one —
she rested her hand on the final card —
represents the future.
What might be or can be or will be
depending on what you choose.
The Ten of Wands means you're carrying a load.
It is heavy and hard to bear,
but you have almost made it.

It is a turning-point card.
A card of opportunity.
One that means it is time to make a choice:
keep carrying what weighs you down,
or set yourself free.

All I could think about was you.

I looked at the women dancing together in my past.
Us.
The royalty gone wrong in my present.
Us.
The woman struggling and all alone in my future.
Would that be one or both of us?
I looked away.

Okay, I said. *Okay.*
Thank you.

* * *

We wandered through the house, holding hands,
and found more destruction
than construction
in the upstairs rooms.
It made me wonder
if we should be wrecking this house:
a place that was already so ruined.

I took in the
storm-shattered windows,
star-shaped holes in the walls,
cracks that splintered like the veins in my arms,
running along the baseboards like blood.

There was a dark stain on the ceiling
that could have been a storm cloud.
Insulation piled in corners like snow.
Broken beams and broken dreams
and all the things this house might have been.

The ghosts of unmade memories
were everywhere.

Are you not having fun? she asked.

It was times like these when I felt the weirdest:
when I was having an existential crisis
without you nearby.

Tarot was supposed to be fun.
Unfinished houses didn't make normal people's
stomachs clench.
Broken glass shouldn't have cut me so deeply
without cutting me at all.

But here I was,
in the middle of a party,
on the verge of panic
because of a weary woman carrying a bundle of sticks
on a card in a pretty girl's pocket.
Because of a tub sitting like an undocked boat
in the center of what might have become a bathroom.
And I wished that I wasn't so affected
by broken, lonely things.

I'm having fun, I almost said.
But I decided I didn't want to lie tonight.
Instead, I pressed my lips against her temple.

I was with her,
but I was wishing for you.
Wishing you were here to bear witness
and be sad too.
And the more I drank,
the more I felt the way these forsaken houses looked:
creaky and hollow and unsure of how to be.

It was getting kind of depressing,
so I sent you a text,
but my phone died before you wrote back.
So I filled and emptied my red cup a few more times
and then I danced with her
until I missed you less.

Right before curfew,
we stepped into a bedroom.
And it only had three walls.
Studs stood like bones
with no sinew or skin or muscle.
But I could tell it would have been the biggest one.

She flicked open her phone's flashlight
and I saw something new through beer-bleary eyes:
Bird nests on the blades of the ceiling fan.
Ivy twisting up the support beams.
Moss on the floor, like a thick green carpet.
Nature taking parts of the skeleton room back.

And something about life snaking its way inside,
even if it wasn't the life the house had expected,
made me feel a tiny bit better.

*   *   *

Under a shattered skylight,
where we could see the moon if we stared straight up,
she and I kissed with abandon.

It wasn't like it was with us,
but it made my belly burn in a way that was
pleasant and unfamiliar.
Her braids were nice to run my fingers through.
And she smelled like summer when it was barely spring.
It was great,
brainless and gentle and freeing,
until she pulled back and said,
I think I really like you.

I smiled and looked down at the spongy moss beneath our feet,
pretending to be shy,
then up at the waxing moon above our heads.
And she laughed, hard,
with her hand on my cheek.

She was from church,
but she read tarot and kissed girls.
She went to private school,
but she partied in abandoned houses.
She looked sweet,
but she was trouble.
I should have liked her back.

I knew I'd never talk to her again.

You were my past, present, and future.
No matter how messy.
No matter how heavy.

And I needed too badly to show
the lonely bathtub,
this sacred, nature-claimed bedroom,
and especially the broken, moon-bright skylight
to you.

14. Her pt. 2

Hey, I say to her.
Hey yourself, she says back.

You look at me.
I look at her.
She looks at you.

And I remember, in that moment,
that I didn't tell you about her
on purpose.

I don't introduce you.
I don't introduce her.
It's awkward as hell, but how do you say to a girl you've kissed,
Yo, this is the girl I love?

    How you been? I ask instead.

Okay.

    Haven't seen you in a while.

Why would you have?

    I . . . guess I deserve that. You skipping too?

She shrugs like, *What does it look like?*
Then crosses her arms and says,
You never texted me back.

      I know. I'm sorry.

No, you aren't.

She's right. I don't say anything.

Because of her? she asks, jerking her chin in your direction.

You take a step forward.
Hey, you say with a smile. *I'm —*

I don't care who you are, she says.
I'm talking to her.
She points at me.

      I say:
      Yeah, okay? Because of her.
      Can we talk somewhere else?
      Or some other time?

She looks at you.
Looks at me.
I don't want to talk to you anymore.

She walks away
and takes all the oxygen in the room with her.
And I'm gasping.
I can't catch my breath.

I hate confrontation more than
I hate telling the truth.

*   *   *

You and I get into it in the parking lot.

What the hell was that? you ask.

  Nothing.

Jesus. Don't lie.

  I'm not.

I'm only asking you one more time.
And then I'll walk or call a car to get home.
What. The fuck. Was that?

  I heave a sigh.
  I kissed her. Then I never spoke to her again.

What the hell? Who does that?

A lot of people actually.

Wow.

Why are you even mad? It's not like I did it to you.

Really? That's what you're gonna say to me right now?

I don't know what you want me to say.
You're a better person than me.

No I'm not.

Would you have rather I kept texting her when I don't have any feelings for her at all?

No. You should have told her the truth.

I look at you.
I think she got the message.

How can you just do that to someone?
How can you be so cold?

You're one to talk.

That stops you.
But then your face turns icy.

We take turns pitching hurts at each other,
and I guess I'm up at bat.
But I don't even swing.
I just stand there and take it.

Well, why didn't you tell me about her?
You're not my girlfriend.
Why would I care about you kissing some other girl?

Of all the things you could say,
this is the one that always sticks to me.
In me.
Like a thorn.

                  Like a needle.

                                    Like a knife.

I say it too sometimes,
just to remind myself of the truth.
I say it over and over and over
until it starts to sound like another language.

        I'm not your girlfriend. I'm not your girlfriend.
            I'm not your girlfriend.
I'mnot yourgirlfriend. I'mnot yourgirlfriend. I'mnot yourgirlfriend.
imnotyourgirlfriendimnotyourgirlfriendimnotyourgirlfriend
            imnotyourgirlfriend

It's a truth I know
but one I can't seem to stomach.

You're not my girlfriend, you spit at me.

Even though you swear you're not mad about me kissing her.

I know I'm not your girlfriend, I whisper.

Like I could ever
fucking
forget.

268 DAYS BEFORE THE FIRE

Was it fun? I asked.

A little.

Are you going to see him again?

Maybe.

Does he still like you?

Seems like it.

Do you still like him?

Kinda.

I bet he loves you.
I bet he wants to marry you and have babies with you.

Fuck you.

I bet you wouldn't say that to him.

You rolled your eyes.

You love to be liked, I said.

So do you.

>*No.*
>*I don't care if people like me. I care if people love me.*
>*And the only person I care about loving me*
>*other than my mom and dad and brother and gran*
>*is you.*

You didn't say anything.

>*I don't think you can handle being actually loved,* I said.

You're such an asshole.

>*Whatever.*
>*You know I'm right.*

You're wrong.
And you're a liar.

>*What do you think I'm lying about?*

Everything!

>*Not everything.*

I'm not an idiot.
I know how much you lie.

I don't lie about anything that matters.

Where were you, then?
That night when you texted.

> *What night when I texted?*
> *I text you every night.*

You know what night.
The same night I was with him.

> I stared at you.

You pulled out your phone.
Scrolled back and back until —
When you sent,
"Sadness is a lonely house inside me.
I'll break every window to escape it
despite the unlocked doors."

> *I was at home,* I lied.

Bullshit.
You're on my case about that guy
when nothing even happened,
and you're being shady as hell,
lying about where you were
on the same night.

Because it doesn't matter.

*Just because it doesn't matter to you doesn't mean it doesn't matter
to me.*

Why does it matter to you?

Everything about you matters to me, you whispered.

I swallowed hard.
Okay.
I'm sorry.
The truth is, I don't want to tell you.

Why?

I don't want to tell you why.

God. You're such a pain in the ass.

So are you.

But how do I know? you asked.
How am I supposed to know
what's true and what isn't?
You lie so often,
so easily and so well.
It confuses me.

I have all these questions but
I can't believe your answers.

> *Ask me a question, I said.*
> *Ask me anything right now.*
> *I'll tell you the truth.*

You crossed your arms.
Looked up.
Looked down.
Looked at me.

How do I know it's true when you say you love me?
How do I know that isn't a lie too?

> I took a deep breath.
> Touched the pearly underside of the seashell in my pocket.
> *It's the truest thing I know.*

But how do I know?

Can't you feel it? I wanted to shout. *Can't you feel me?*
Can't you see it? I wanted to scream. *Can't you see me?*

> My voice broke.
> *You know what you do to my head.*
> *To my heart.*

The truth was
I wanted to write you a poem the length of a skyscraper.
To play you a year's worth of the most perfect music.
To bake you dozens of gourmet desserts
and bring you baskets of wildflowers
and buy you new boots and books, bracelets and bags.
I wanted to hold you while you were sleeping,
from dusk till dawn,
even if it meant I didn't sleep at all.

I wanted to keep you safe.

The truth was
maybe I didn't know what it meant to love someone.
Or maybe I just didn't know what words to say.
But I knew that the colors of sunrise and sunset
and the sun itself reminded me of your warmth,
even when you were being as cold and as distant
as the dark side of the moon.

I knew that I wanted you every hour of every day,
no matter where I was or who else I was with.
And I knew that my heart was yours,
whether you decided to take it and hold it close
or leave it, bleeding and barely beating.

All of that had to add up to something.

I guess you either believe me,
I said,
or
you don't.

A lie:

"You're not my girlfriend."

The truth?
We both know exactly what I am.
What you are.
Who we are to each other.

We are great friends and messy sweethearts.
We are offbeat oddballs and melancholy misfits.
We are imperfect but we are still perfect.
I am your person.
And you are mine.

But yeah, fine.
I guess if you want to get technical.
If you want to talk about this whole thing
as if it were a business arrangement
with a missing contract,
I'm not exactly your girlfriend.

But if you counted up the hours I spent thinking of you
and the days we spent in your basement bedroom.
If you measured the ways we've touched
and the things we've said.
If you weigh the promise that I will always be here
or somewhere, loving you?
I'm definitely not your girlfriend.

152

I am enduringly and irrevocably
way, way more
than that.

15. You the ocean and me

These are our last few hours of freedom, I say.
Let's just be mad tomorrow.

Slowly, you uncross your arms.
I swallow my hurt
and I'm sure you choke down some of your own.
You nod
and I smile.

We go to the beach.

The sun is already setting,
and it's getting even colder.
I blast the heat in my brother's truck
so high it rattles.
But it's worth it to keep you warm.

We're too quiet.
I'm worried the whole ride will be awkward,
that we won't recover after the fight in the parking lot
and the rest of the day will be ruined.
But then I play that savage and somber song
from this morning.
I turn it up bit by bit,
hoping it can be a soft and slow salvation.

You smirk at me,
then scramble through the sliding back window of the cab
before I even realize it's happening.

I have no idea what you're doing,
but I slow down a little to help you balance.
To hold you steady.
To keep you safe.

I turn the music up louder.

When I glance at your reflection in the rearview mirror,
you could be a siren standing there.
But sirens are never lucky enough
to be blessed with brown skin and bright scarves,
black hair flying skyward and darkly wet eyes.
Somehow, I still manage to pay attention to the road,
but I'm grinning wide.

You reenact the "we are infinite" tunnel scene
from *Perks* (another one of our favorites).
And just as the chorus crescendos,
you lift your arms and fling them open,
and your mouth, it's screaming.

And this is how we apologize
when words aren't enough:
me with music, you with madness.

The wind is howling, and I'm laughing so hard I'm crying,
and you are shivering like crazy
by the time you climb back inside.

I love you, I say,
and I don't mean it in the way that's
always too much because it's too true.
I mean it like, *I loved that.*
Like, *You're so ballsy and brave.*
Like:
You're better than everyone I have ever known.

Worth it? I ask.

Yup, you say. *But gimme your jacket.*
And even though I'm cold too, I do.

*   *   *

The first order of business
when we get to the beach
is to hot box the shit out of the truck.

We only have to take a few big pulls
before the cab is thick with smoke
like San Francisco fog,
white and swirling and alive.

This time of year,
there is no evening.
And that is especially true today.
Afternoon sinks into night
instantly —
light just tripping and
falling into the dark.

And so soon,
too soon,
we're swallowed by blackness.

It's so weird that the moon,
like,
controls the ocean,
I say as soon as the high hits.

I know, you say.
Like,
is the moon the ocean's dad or something?
And I know you're elevated too.

We giggle. A lot.
Then climb out of the truck.
We walk out onto the bumpy sand arm in arm,
floating.

We stand close enough to the rocks
to hear the water when it hits.
And it's freezing, so we hold each other close
and keep smoking.

I clutch the joint, because you refuse to take off your gloves.
Press my freezing fingertips to your lips,
then mine,
then to yours again.

Did you know it's the winter solstice? I ask.

Today? you say.

Yep.

Badass, you mutter.
And then we don't say anything for a while.

You're high,
so you do that thing where you start asking
impossible-to-answer questions.
You always zone out right before it happens,
so I know it's coming when you get quiet.

You're silent for a beat too long, so I glance over.
See that you're staring at the end of the joint.
It is bright red and burning,
a glowing dot in the growing dark.

Would fire exist if oxygen didn't?

You look out at the ocean.

What about water?

And if water didn't exist, what would earth be like?

What would humans?

If we didn't breathe oxygen because it didn't exist, who would we
*   even be?*

What would we look like?

Would we have hair? Or eyeballs? Cuticles or organs?

Would we need lungs if we didn't need to breathe? What about
*   hearts?*

Would we even have blood since blood is, like, mostly water?

And if we didn't have blood, would we have bones?

Would we be, like, weird, boneless aliens?

You let out an enormous gasp.

Wait. WAIT.

Are aliens

*   just humans*

*   who live in places*

*   where oxygen doesn't exist?*

*   I think we should sit down, I say.*

You nod.

We settle into the cold, soft sand.

We're quiet.
But it's different than it was in the car.
More private. More peaceful.
More empty but also
more full.

I lean against you, and you lean against an old rotted-out piece of
    driftwood.
We hold hands and listen to the waves
and I start thinking about colors.

About the vivid green of my grandmother's front door.
The angry red of the bridge.
The tranquil violet of your lavender scented candles.
And then, because we're at the beach,
I think about
the everywhere blue
from the day I almost died.

Blue is a strange color, I say out loud.
Thinking of my grandmother calling me a blue, golden girl.
I think of water and sky and white people's eyes.

The world would love us to believe that blue eyes are the prettiest:
"Her eyes were blue as the sea," authors write;
"Blue as the sky," singers sing;
"Blue as sapphires, shining bright,"
like they're all saying something new.

But it's like they don't think about what happens to all that blue shit
in the dark.

I have this thought. And it is dark. And then I look over at you.
At your eyes.

And they're
the ocean sparkling, like spilled oil at midnight.
The black sky flickering with a hundred thousand stars.
Every gemstone imaginable catching the glint of the moon
and shattering those tiny bits of light into a million pieces
that shimmer in the shadows.

I want to say this, all of this, to you,
that your dark eyes are better than every blue eye I've ever seen.
But I don't know how to without sounding ridiculous.

My head is doing that thing it always does
when I'm high:
thoughts racing ahead and leaving me behind.

I tuck a curl behind your ear,
stare for too long and wait for you to ask,
What?

Then I shake my head, look away.
I take a deep breath, like I always have to
before I tell the truth.

Run my cold fingers along the bit of your wrist that's showing,
because my pockets are empty.
(You're the only treasure I brought with me tonight.)

I say:
Nothing.
You're just gorgeous as hell.
Even in the dark.

When you kiss me,
I just remind myself to breathe.

* * *

We sit there for as long as we can,
no one but
you the ocean and me.
And right before we leave, you whisper:
Today was like us.

I know exactly what you mean.

We so often start out raging,
like we're made of hot hate and heat.
We're unpredictable, unmanageable, unrestrained,
like the back lot dumpster fire
we started at dawn.

But
almost always
we end up here:
Tired and together.
Close and quiet and crashing,
like the wild waves on this empty beach.
Feeling savage and somber.
Clinging to each other
in the dark.

963 DAYS BEFORE THE FIRE

When I was in eighth grade
I tried going out with a boy.
I thought it was what I was supposed to do.

He asked me to a dance,
I said yes,
and I wore an ocean-blue dress.
But once we were there,
I didn't know where to put my hands.

With girls it was easy,
even back then.
My fingers naturally slipped into their hair,
tucked into their pockets,
hooked into their belt loops,
landed on their (nonexistent) hips.

I was so used to touching my friends
that touching the people I wanted to be
a little more than friends with
was simple:
I was the same as I always was
with a little extra on top.

But boys were different.
And this boy touched me a lot

before I could even figure out
if I wanted him touching me at all.

So we were sitting.
And he was touching my hands
and my shoulders
and my thighs
when I finally said, *Wanna dance?*
just so I could have the space
I didn't know how to ask for.

But the worst thing that could have happened next,
when a girl is fourteen
and at her first dance
and standing in front of a boy,
happened.

My period arrived unannounced,
moist and sticky against the back of my dress
like I'd sat on a bench that was missing
its WET PAINT sign,
like something violent and irreversible had happened
in the ocean of my body.

He squealed and pointed and everyone looked.
And in that moment
I was reminded
of so many things.

That
anatomy was complicated
and I was still learning how all the parts of me worked.

That
desperation for acceptance
could make people so casually cruel.

That
I didn't know how to love someone
who was disgusted by this cosmic cycle.
Because blood would spill from my body
whenever the moon decided it was time.

That
women were like the sea: Always shifting.
Stormy and calm and crashing and quiet.
Able to hold and house and carry things with ease.
Always gorgeous but in infinite ways.
We moved with the moon.

Men, on the other hand, were too often like land:
sturdy and solid
but unable to change
without seismic destruction.

That
I would never go out
with someone like him again.

I'd always been obsessed with water.
Solid ground would never be enough.

* * *

I cried that night as I told my mother what had happened.
That it made me know
without a doubt who I was.

She listened as she drew me a bath.
Filled the tub with water
and made it smell sweet
with lavender and vanilla.

And once my hair was down and the soiled dress cast aside,
once I was in, sunk low and shoulders-deep,
knees peaking like narrow, brown mountains,
she said:
Nothing you accept about yourself can be used against you to diminish
    you.
One of my favorite poets, Audre Lorde, wrote that.

And with that one sentence,
that single line,
I knew she understood.
She saw me.
I closed my eyes, content with seeing nothing for a while,
and sighed.

When I climbed out of the bath,
a glass of champagne that sparkled with drinkable stars
was waiting for me
in a tall, thin glass
as curveless as my body.

She read me a poem by Lucille Clifton
called "wishes for sons."
More wise words from wise women
to fortify this new version of me.

And then,
with as much tenderness as she'd told me
that my heart and my body
wasn't wrong,
she showed me how to get the moon's gentle urging that I was all
    grown up now
out of intricate, delicate,
ocean-blue lace.

16. Love-drunk

We're silent on the ride back to school to pick up your car,
high still hovering like low-hanging clouds.

I play music that fits our late afternoon:
it is tender and truthful,
haunting and hungry.
You hum along with your eyes closed,
slipping in and out of sleep.

I focus on the road.
It is long and winding and empty,
but rush hour is rushing toward us.
Our parents will be off soon,
along with the rest of the state.
And all that matters now is beating the traffic
and them
home.

We say goodbye around the corner from the back lot.
We don't want to fully return to the scene of our crime.
You touch my cheek.
I kiss your forehead.
We each look into the dark pools of the other's eyes
like we're trying to find something.
We're a little bit lost.

Call me later? I ask.
Sure, you answer.
You slide out of the truck
like blood,
leaving a stain on my memory of the day,
and it spreads like a wound under cotton.
It won't ever wash out.

I drive home and slip into my brother's bedroom.
Tell him about my whole day
as if I'm writing the story of us:
giving our chaotic choices
and wild wanderings
a beginning,
middle,
and end.

Sounds messy, he says.
Isn't everything? I ask,
thinking of smoke swirling like fog
and the starry, unpredictable universe.
Thinking of waves crashing against rocks
and sloppy, high kisses
and feelings (so many feelings).

And fire. I'm always thinking about fire.

He bites his bottom lip.
True, he agrees.

My parents get home late,
easing the door open together.
They are love-drunk
and maybe a little real-drunk,
and they are more tipsy than tough
as they tell me
they discussed my punishment over dinner.

It's their anniversary.
I had forgotten.
I feel like the worst daughter
on the face of the earth.

We decided, my father says,
that you can keep your phone,
your computer,
the TV in your room.

But you can say goodbye, my mother tags herself in,
to most of what
you wanted for Christmas.

I wonder if this is what it is to be a parent:
More talking than kissing when you're on a date.
More presence than presents as the years pass
like minutes.

Okay, I say.
Because what else is there to say?
I set a fire
on the same day
twenty years ago
when my parents vowed to stay
in love.

* * *

I text you and you don't text back.
I call you, and it rings only twice before you send me
and everything I have to say
to voicemail.

I text you again. Then I feel stupid.
I put my phone down and walk into another room.

I just saw you, just spent the whole day with you.
I spoke to you more than anyone else for the last twelve hours.
Still, I'm panicky about an unanswered text.
I'm anxious wondering why you've just ignored my call.

This is a part of the problem:
I want you too desperately.
I see it and I feel it and I can't stop it.
However much I have of you
it's never, ever enough.

I eat ice cream and you don't text.
I watch TV and you don't call.
I rearrange the treasures that litter my dresser by size
and touch the stolen stone heart still hidden under my bed.
I scroll and like and post and even then,
nothing.
So I make my parents a collage.

I chop up tiny bits of paper
the same color as browned butter for their skin.
I shred images of the night sky for my mother's hair
and guide the scissors through pages filled with trees
and tall grass and fields of wildflowers
until I find enough dark green for my father's favorite suit.

When I finish, I scribble *happy anniversary* on the back,
slide it under their door like a secret,
wash my glue-sticky hands.

I take a shower.
Smooth lotion over my skin like paint.
Step into peach fuzz–soft pajamas.

I miss you.

I miss you, but I'm grateful for the distance.
Grateful for my hands and the comfort of art.
Grateful for love and the slow but steady passage of time.

Grateful to be reminded that there are so many beautiful things in
    the world
other than us.

Still,
I shimmy under my sheets wishing for the warmth of your body in
    my bed,
wishing the collage of my thoughts
wasn't so often
(wasn't almost always)
a messy tapestry of you.

I fall asleep
holding my phone
like all my wanting:
tight and close.
Right up against my gently beating heart.

A lie (you told me):

"Just because you love someone doesn't mean you get to have
   them."

The truth?
         You had me,
                  but I didn't have you.

So I guess it wasn't a lie.

I just didn't want to believe it.

921 DAYS BEFORE THE FIRE

Eighth grade was when you had your first kiss.

You told me that, one day,
after a white boy in your class pulled at your bra strap
and let it spring back, hard and stinging, against your skin,
a girl walked right over to him and kneed him in the balls.

You told me that the girl got in trouble.
Got suspended, because of some zero-tolerance policy
that seemed to apply to Black girls
more often than it did to white boys.

The boy, he'd been popping your bra strap
like the D string on the double bass he played in orchestra
for weeks.
And you'd been telling him to stop,
slapping his hand away,
shouting at him not to come near you at all.

Every week, you'd shrink a little more from his touch,
as your indignance seemed to egg him on.
As your anger seemed to amuse him.

And this girl, you said, had been watching all along.
Had been keeping a tally of how many times
your *no*
wasn't listened to.

You'd noticed her noticing you.
It made you want to hide.
But she'd just kept watching,
kept keeping score.
Deciding on her own to keep you safe.

When you went to her house,
the day of the suspension,
you hadn't planned what you'd say.

And when she opened the door, you said,
looking butch and beautiful,
I completely lost my way.

She wore short cornrows and baggy jeans and
glasses that were a little bent from fighting.
She had a single deep dimple stitched into her left cheek
and lashes as long as your fingernails.

She told you about the counting,
showed you the tally in her notebook.
Told you that that day, he'd popped your strap
one too many times for her to take.

You stood there, remembering
how she'd protected you.
How she'd been so brave.
How she'd made the boy cry.

You grinned, and she grinned,
and you licked your lips while staring,
without blinking,
at hers.

You stepped closer and whispered,
Can I kiss you?
And then the girl said yes.

You had only seen kissing on TV,
but, you told me, you did your absolute best.

As you kissed,
you imagined her tally was of your failures,
not his transgressions.
You imagined her seeing you as helpless,
which made you feel hopeless.
In your imagination, she kicked the boy again and again,
and each time felt delicious.

But her kindness sank into your heart like a knife.

Just as the kiss ended,
you reared back and slapped her.
Her eyes filled with tears and she punched you in the gut,
left you doubled over in her front yard.

I can take care of myself, you screamed
at her closed front door,
then, years later,
at me.
But unlike the butch, beautiful girl,
I am not trying to save you.

I am only
(I am always)
trying to love you.

17. Like a bomb

It's well after midnight when your text arrives,
lighting up my phone
like a bomb
in the dark.

I need you
is all it says.

So I come running.

240 DAYS BEFORE THE FIRE

I made this for you.

I held out a tiny treasure chest I'd found at a thrift shop.
I'd covered it in the smallest seashells
and fractured sea glass
and sequins from my collection —
trinkets I'd saved over the years that reminded me to breathe.

You took it like it might shatter.
Held it like you might hurt it.
For me? you asked, turning it over in your hands.
I nodded.

Why?

I didn't need a reason to give you beautiful things.
But you wanted a reason, so I told you one of many.

Because sometimes I think you don't get it,
the way I feel about you.
And today I felt brave enough to show you.

I pointed to the seashells, the sea glass, the sequins.
Then I pointed to the sky.

If you ever doubt how I feel,
count the ripples on every seashell on this box.
Count the pieces of sea glass,
count the sequins,
then count the stars.
That number is how long I'll love you.
In seconds,
minutes,
hours,
and days.

You looked at me like I was speaking French.

That's why.

A truth:

We let the believing go.
Let the love lie.
Let the truth live without the words as its heartbeat.

I didn't tell you I loved you anymore
as I pulled your head into my lap,
as I stroked your untamable, impossible hair.

You didn't write it in the countless poems
you scribbled on rough brown paper,
weighed down with smooth stones,
and left by my front door.

I didn't say it when I was sad,
and you refused to say it when you were angry.
But we both knew that inexpressible desire was the reason
behind my torrents of tears;
that uncontainable affection
was why you were so quick to rage.

Since I couldn't say it when I wanted to,
how I wanted to,
I said it with handmade jewelry and wildflowers,
long hugs and longer night drives.

Since you couldn't bear to hear it,
couldn't bear to know it was true,
you said it with soft touches and softer secrets,
with rare pieces of sea glass and seashells
(things I loved, from a place I loved)
overflowing in your hands.

I love you, we said
in big and small ways.
But because you didn't believe me,
couldn't believe me,
and your lack of faith cut into my chest
deep and deadly,
we said it with choices
instead of letters or voices.

And for as long as I live, I'll regret it.
Not making sure you knew what was true.

I wish I'd been brave enough to demand that you hear it,
see it,
feel it.
(Even when you refused to listen.)

18. Anywhere

When I get to your house
you're standing outside waiting for me.

Tight jeans and combat boots.
Black skin smooth enough to blend,
like a shadow,
into the night.

Your hair is trembling in the wind
as fiercely as a match lit with dark flames:
you'll either burn out quick
or start a wildfire.

Sometimes your beauty catches me off guard,
makes my breath catch in my chest.
It is so undeniable.
It is completely absolute.

Like earlier, on the way to the beach.
Like in your basement, on my sixteenth birthday.
Like this morning in the car
and yesterday
and probably tomorrow, too.
This is one of those moments.

You slide into the truck while I'm still relearning the art of
    breathing.

I don't ask what happened
and you don't tell.
You just say: *Let's go anywhere.*

I take in your sad, dark eyes,
toss my arm across your shoulders,
throw the truck in reverse,
and say, *Okay.*

226 DAYS BEFORE THE FIRE

You had a soft side that you tried to hide.
A part of you that loved love
and loved loving
and loved to be loved in return.

A part of you that wasn't too afraid to want it;
was brave enough to take it
when it was right in front of you.

The first time you let yourself be soft
with me,
it seemed that the softness gave you freedom.
You leaned back and relaxed your body against mine
where we lay on your bright yellow sheets.
You closed your eyes and let my fingers get lost in your curls.
You let your guard down, and for just a second,
I could see what it would be like if you really did it.
If you let me love you.

But that kind of softness? It stole something from you too.
Something essential to your being.
Something that kept you (and maybe me) safe.

And so, when the moment had passed,
when you sat up and moved away from me,
your wall building itself back up brick by brick

with jokes and confidence and distance,
I swallowed hard and let it happen.

I was always so full of feeling that I knew what it was like
to have to keep so much of yourself
to yourself.
To feel like you had to stop it when it started to seep out.

People like us had to be careful.
Or we could cause earthquakes.
Hurricanes.
Tsunamis
of feeling.

It could swallow us whole.

19. Temple Heights

For the whole drive,
there is far-off lightning in the dark sky,
blinking and bright behind even darker clouds:
a flickering candle casting shadows
in a faraway, empty room.

It looks like the night is keeping a secret.
So I show you one of mine.

This is where I went,
I tell you when we get there.
The night I texted you about
sadness being a house.

Here? you ask, smirking.
Temple Heights? you ask, frowning.
Why would you come here? you ask, quieting.

I park and point to the trees.
Let me show you.

199 DAYS BEFORE THE FIRE

I had a dark side.
One I didn't want anyone to see.
I was more comfortable being soft,
being hurt,
being scared,
instead of hard
or reckless
or cruel.

But you saw it
one day when I was angry at the world.
When it felt like everyone wanted something different from me.

My dad wanted a kid who loved the Lord.
My teachers wanted a student who turned things in on time.
My brother wanted me to stop being so intense,
and my mother wanted me to be okay with my own intensity.

I didn't know how to love a God who let Bad Things happen.
I couldn't stop thinking about all the Bad Things long enough to
    finish my homework.
I couldn't help the fact that Bad Things hit me hard
and knocked me hollow.
And I didn't know how to accept feeling it all, all the time.

Everyone wanted something from me
except you.

I fought with my parents and took my brother's truck.
Drove to your house and stormed through your wooded backyard,
smashing and crashing and disturbing the peace.

You asked me what was wrong, but everything was wrong.
Because there were days
when I felt my pain
and your pain
and the pain of all the Bad Things in the world.
And how could I say that without having to explain?
And how could I explain?

I had come to your house
but I wanted to be alone.
So I said what I knew would make you leave me
alone.

> *How can someone like you help someone like me?*
> *I said, my voice dripping venom.*

What does that mean?

> *It means we're both a mess.*

Right. So maybe I can help you.
Maybe if you tell me, I'll understand.

I laughed.
Nah. You can't help.
You're way more fucked up than me.

My words still haunt me.
Remembering your face that day makes me want to fall to pieces.
And the way you walked away without looking back . . .

You saw how I could turn,
how I could harm:
Cut with my words.
Tear with my teeth.
Break with my body.

Maybe that was why you resisted letting yourself go with me.
Maybe that was why I wanted you to.

I knew the only way to kill the darkness in me
was to flood it with light.

20. The smallest lies

There was a party, I say.
That girl from the movie theater?
She brought me here
to go to a party.

The houses are all dark as shadows.
Stoic stone ghosts nestled in the trees.
You reach for my hand as I reach out to open the front door.

(I tell you to hold me tight.
You don't let go.)

I give you a tour, pretending I'm a real estate agent.
I point out the starburst holes in the walls,
the shattered windows,
the crumbling fireplace,
like they're amenities on a wish list.

I run my hand over the dusty counters
in the war-torn kitchen.
Slam a white handprint onto the thigh of my black jeans.
Granite? you ask.
Marble, I say.
Oh my. Even better.

We go upstairs slowly,
steam rising from our mouths in white clouds as we talk.
You worry about spiders and rats and snakes,
but I tell you they'll all run when they hear us coming.
And even if they don't, I say, *I'll keep them away.*

When I shine my phone's light toward the lonely tub, I ask,
Doesn't it look like a boat?
You walk right up to it and climb inside.
Gesture as if you're yanking on ropes and tying knots,
casting an invisible sail before sitting down slow and
leaning way, way back.

I grin and sink in with you,
stick my butt right between your limitless legs.
And I want to stay here forever
in our makeshift, porcelain raft,
where we can be close and quiet,
gentle and tired.

This reminds me of that scene from Pretty Woman, I say.

That movie would have been so much better if she'd been gay.

I nod, pressing my head back against the front of your shoulder,
and you settle, with your arms, loose and lingering,
around my waist.
We breathe slow and steady,
slow and steady.

Why didn't you tell me about her? you whisper after a while.

And I sigh because I thought we were done with this.

And if we aren't, how can I tell you the truth?

How do I say,

"*She showed me cards for my past, present, and future, and all I could
    see was you.*

I kissed her, and I liked it, but it didn't change a thing.

I was mad at you. I am mad at you. I am madly in love with you.

She is so beautiful, so kind, so weird and cool, but none of it matters.

(And I think things like that should matter.)

Not much matters, though, when I compare anything to you"?

How do I say,

"*I didn't tell you because*

I couldn't tell you because

I can't say anything true without choking because

I am always terrified"?

Do I say,

"*I didn't tell you because my heart is the size of the earth,*

but you could split it open with one look.

I can't risk a hemorrhage that would drown the whole world"?

I trace a pattern on your thigh with the tip of my finger
as I lie.

I don't know, I say. *Didn't seem like a big deal.*
You swallow and I feel your neck move like a snake against my
    temple.
I cover your hands, where they rest on my belly, with my own.

I don't want to be this way, but the truth makes
my head and heart and mouth feel stuffed with cotton —
too full to speak.

Okay, you say. And I can't tell if you believe me. *Okay.*

(Do you think they call the smallest lies

white

because they're so blinding?)

A lie:

"All you need is love."

The truth:
you need a hell of a lot more
than that.

153 DAYS BEFORE THE FIRE

Someone hurt you.
Left you with a cut lip and a bruised cheek
because you'd said something that was too much for them to
    handle,
something too true that they didn't want to hear.

You wouldn't tell me who because you knew what would happen.
The way I would cry.
The way I would riot.
The way I would hunt them down and hurt them back.

I handled it, you told me.
And I believed you, but I wanted to handle it too.

Don't look like that, you said next.

      Like what?

Like it happened to you.

I didn't know how to tell you that that was the way it felt.
That whenever you hurt, I hurt.
That your pain was mine, too.
Not figuratively.
Literally.

(You wouldn't have believed the way my cheek throbbed.)
(I could almost taste my own penny-flavored blood.)

It did, though, I said, balling my fists inside my sleeves,
my whole being aching like a tooth.
It happened to me, too.

I know, you said.
And I knew the only way you could know
was if
my hurt took up residence in your body
the same way yours made a home inside me.

So shut up, I said, crying a little.

You laughed.

21. Half-full

When I lean forward to retie my shoe,
you lean half your body out of the tub to open the toilet.

You light up your phone to peek inside.
You glance back at me, grinning.

What? I say,
wondering what could possibly be in a toilet
in an abandoned house
that would make you smile like that.

You pull out a half-full (half-empty?)
bottle of whiskey
and lift it above your head like it's a trophy.

898 DAYS BEFORE THE FIRE

The end of freshman year was hard for you.

You grew three inches in three months.
You started getting curves everywhere you didn't have them
only weeks (minutes?) before.
You quit gymnastics after your coach told you that
most gymnasts were under five-three;
most weighed so much less than this new you.

It was one thing to feel like a stranger in your own body.
Girls are used to that.
It was quite another to have someone else,
someone male,
tell you that you'd lost control of something.
What he couldn't see
is that you'd always been powerless against it.

Little girls' bodies are war zones with no allies.
And women are made of whatever survives.

You went from a flat horizon to a mountainous landscape.
A pole to a vase.
A straight shot to a road full of sharp turns and yellow caution signs.

Simplistic to complicated. Safe to dangerous.

And everyone noticed, including me.

But I didn't know you yet.

22. You're always right

You take a sip and pass the bottle to me.
I take one too, then pass it back to you.
My chest burns and it makes you cough,
but the whiskey is just a means to an end.

We seek oblivion,
and we'll get there no matter what it takes.

We play a game we made up called Celebrity Age,
and you are so wrong
so often
that you get drunk quick.

> *How old is Danny DeVito?*

Fifty-five?

> *I'm gonna guess he's way older than that. I say seventy-three.*
> I search it. Seventy-seven.
> *You're not even close,* I say. I win.

You drink.

> *What about Molly Ringwald?* I ask.

Like forty-something maybe.

Bro, she was making movies in the eighties. She's *probably*
    fifty-five.
I search it. *She's fifty-four,* I say. I'm closer, so
you drink.

We guess and search and sip until we get bored.
Then I play the savage and somber song on my phone,
and we dance together in the messy, half-finished bathroom.

We move into the bedroom because I still haven't shown you the
    skylight.
Haven't shown you how nature is snaking its way in.
And when I do,
when I point to where the bird nests were,
to where the moss still is,
to where you can look straight up and see stars, you say,

It's a temple. It's the temple in Temple Heights.

Because what is a temple?
A special place.
A peaceful place.
A holy and sacred space.

You're right, I say.
I sit on the mossy carpet and you sit across from me,
quarter-full whiskey bottle between our knees.

You're always right,
except at guessing celebrity ages.

Ha-ha, you say.

I can barely see you,
but I can see you enough to know I want to kiss you.
Right here and now
in this temple of ours.

I lean forward, too eager and too drunk
in the too-deep dark.

My knee
knocks
into
the whiskey.

The bottle topples over and spills beside us,
an amber puddle that snakes into the floor's cracks
like it's running
away.

A truth:

It grated on me,
all the silence.
How we tiptoed around what was happening
in our stormy chests,
in our wind-whipped hearts.

It obliterated us to hold hands
and let go.
Tormented us to sit so closely
only to be forced apart.
It made us ache to say things we didn't mean.
But we said them
to bury, to drown, to hide
all the unsaid things we did.

And if we were the sea,
the truth was a piece of broken glass.
We swallowed it whole,
its sharp edges becoming cutting remarks,
and returned it to shore,
silent, salt-smooth, and see-through,
a safe treasure to keep forever when it used to be
discarded and dangerous.

Or maybe the truth was the ocean
and we were the old, shattered pieces of a wine bottle,
the chunks of window from ancient shipwrecks,
hoping to be saved.

But I'm too tumbled and turned around —
too seasick and surrendered.
And you're tossed aside,
choking on the relentless waves of us.

The truth remains
a stunning and powerful
ocean of feeling,
swelling and rushing with
endless ripples of love.

The truth remains
what it always was,
what it always will be:
completely unchanged.

888 DAYS BEFORE THE FIRE

It was the middle of summer after freshman year
when I decided I wasn't going back to school.

Everyone was always looking at me
(at my clothes, at my hair),
but no one really saw who I was.
Nobody else seemed to be hurting,
but everything from packed hallways to casual cruelty made me
    ache.
I felt like I was all alone
because I wasn't like *them*.

I couldn't sit in that building, in those classrooms, in my skin any
    longer.
And I told my mother I wasn't going back.

Don't be ridiculous, she said.
You have to go to school.
But maybe next year you'll make a friend.

I planned to spend all summer outlining the merits of home-
    schooling.

But
twenty-one days later,
I met you.

23. Violence delights you

I thought you'd be pissed.
But you're not.
You lean forward the rest of the way,
closing the space that's left between us.

Your lips taste like a campfire,
smoky in a way that is too on the nose to be real.
Then I remember the whiskey.
The smell of it is everywhere,
and sometimes, especially when I'm drunk,
my senses get all mixed up.

I'm sorry, I say, pointing to the spilled booze.
I'm sorry, forgive me?
You nod. You do.
I am messy, sloppy, as I kiss you more,
but the next time we break away,
I reach into my pocket, remembering.

I pull out a joint,
thin and white and wrapped tight.
An apology because the whiskey has been wasted
but we aren't quite wasted enough.

You smile, and I'm so happy to see you smile,
and I'm drunk so I say it,

truths slipping out like
sand between my fingers.

I love making you smile.

You're drunk, you say.
So are you, I say.
(I can tell by the way you've gotten quiet.
By the way you are looking at me like you can't help it.)

So what, you say, not taking your big, black eyes off me.
Your eyelashes flutter a little when you blink.
We both crack up.

You open your lighter,
light the joint.
But instead of flipping it closed,
you flip it around in your hands,
doing tricks you learned on the internet.
You run your palm over the open flame
in that way that makes me nervous.

You probably do this all the time
(this kind of violence delights you),
just not in front of me.
And I don't want to watch it.
Can't watch it.
I need you to stop.

Don't do that, I say.

I don't want you to get burned.

Your skin is so perfect.

I can't watch you mess it up.

Stop fucking around.

You laugh and dance away from me.

And then, in slow motion,

you trip over a piece of broken drywall.

You fall,

and the lighter does too.

121 DAYS BEFORE THE FIRE

Did you know you smell like rose petal ice cream? you asked.

They make rose petal ice cream?

Yep.

Oh. No, I didn't know, I said.
Did you know you smell like roses and smoke?

Really?

Yeah.

That's weird.

Is it? I asked.

I think it's weird, you said. *That we both smell like roses, I mean.
Without even trying.
You, like the pieces that fall away when they're dying,
but mixed with something creamy and sweet.
Me, like if someone brought a valentine bouquet to a bonfire.*

And tossed it in, I added.

You looked at me.

Yeah. I guess it is weird.

24. Smother it

The fire starts small.
And for a second, I think it will die out quickly.

I jump up, reach for your hand,
pull you away, and shove you into the space where the room is
    missing a wall.
I stomp on the tiny blaze, because I saw that in some movie once.
But it doesn't work.

The flames race along the trail of the whiskey spill
and there's too much shit on the floor in here.
Drywall and wooden beams and paper and insulation.
And I wonder why we build the places we live
out of stuff
that so easily catches fire.

Smother it, I think.
We have no water, so we have to smother it.
And I can't get your high questions from the afternoon out of my
    head:
If oxygen didn't exist, would fire?
Would water?

But none of that matters now.

Gimme your jacket, I say.
And you rip it off, like a Band-Aid.

A lie (or maybe a prayer):

"This will work."

103 DAYS BEFORE THE FIRE

We wrote down secrets on strips of paper as thin as ribbons,
slipped them into a clear plastic box I'd found on the beach,
added tiny broken seashells and flat wishing stones,
and buried it all in my backyard.

We made plans to dig it up in five or ten or fifteen years,
a promise that promised we'd be in each other's lives indefinitely,
a heedless hope I clung to.

Because sometimes it felt like you were always trying to say
    goodbye to me.
And I didn't know what to do about it.

So I closed my eyes against the persistent truth of our impossibility,
crossed my fingers,
and wrote one sentence over and over on tiny bits of paper
that I buried with the hope that damp dirt
and heavy rocks and the relentlessness of time
would make it come true:

I wish for forever with you.

25. This is hell

When I was thirteen, I almost died.
Now I'm nearly seventeen and it's happening again.
First by water,
now by fire,
and I remember my father saying that in the Bible
those are the two ways
God destroys the world.

Am I the world? I think as the fire grows,
and then,
Why does God want to destroy me?

And I don't know if this is what they mean
when they say your life flashes before your eyes,
but I start to see my parents and my brother and my gran.
Myself at twelve and thirteen and fourteen and fifteen.
And you.

Your long-fingered hands and painted nails.
Your dark skin and thick thighs.
The way your hair curls at your temples.
You are heaven.
But this is hell.

I throw the jacket over the flames
and it burns away like it's nothing.

We have to go, you say.

81 DAYS BEFORE THE FIRE

How does it feel, to be you? you asked.

You were always asking me these kinds of questions.
Questions no one had ever asked me before.
Questions that maybe no one had ever asked themselves.
Questions that felt like you were trying to see a part of me
that no one else had ever seen.

I always tried my best to answer.

I don't know, I said.
Maybe it feels a bit like fog?
Cloudy in a way it shouldn't be,
making it harder for everyone to see.
Like,
I'm the fog.
Hovering and getting in the way,
making everyone's day a little more gray.
And we're all waiting for the sun to come up.
For the sun to burn me away.

You're not fog, you said instantly.
Or if you are, you're the kind that makes things hazy and beautiful.
The kind that photographers wake up early to capture.
The kind that keeps prey safe.

You're only gray like the moon —
almost silver.
Precious and perfect and shiny.
Like jewelry. Like stars.

I bit my lip to keep from crying.

You answer, then, I said.
What does it feel like to be you?

You had been sitting close to me,
thighs kissing, knuckles knocking,
but before you answered, you stood up and crossed the room.

I saw a video once of a tree that had been struck by lightning.
It was burning on the inside, full of, like,
these crazy swirling flames
while the outside looked completely normal.
When you glanced up, your eyes were glassy but fierce.
That's what it feels like, you said.
To be me.

And before I could flip your insides the way you'd flipped mine
(from something hard to hold, hard to look at too closely,
to something gorgeous),
you said you had to go.

You left.

A truth:

I was growing tired of having the same fights.
I was growing tired of you running away.
I was growing tired of feeling that I wasn't enough.
I was growing tired.
And you were too.

But there were still moments
when my feelings for you were astonishing.
When the way you said my name made me breathless with want.
When you laughed or smiled
or tossed that head of yours in that one particular way
and I couldn't imagine giving you up.

I could imagine something clicking.
Something being reset in the mechanics of us
in just the right moment.
And you'd take my hand
and whisper the only words I'd ever wanted to hear you say.

We'd lie close, limb over limb,
or run wild with nothing to lose
because you had me and I finally had you
and nothing else mattered.

So we were growing tired.
Growing heavy with the maddening weight of
whatever was holding us together.
But we weren't yet tired of trying.

Because even though there was a black hole sucking at you or me
or the concept of our "we,"
there was also a galaxy blooming between us.

And the limitless space between the stars
filled me and you with enough hope to not yet give up
on the thin-as-string possibility
of us.

26. A sudden savior

We make it outside, and I expect you to run.
But you never do what I expect you to.
You grab my hand and look up at the burning bedroom.
Our temporary temple.
And something about the moment feels holy.

We have to bear witness, you say.
We have to stay.

And I don't know why,
but I feel it too:
This desperate need to see how it all ends.
The need to be here when it does.

When the fire spreads to the next room,
flames flying like caged birds suddenly set free,
you let out a primal scream.
I think there's something wild inside you
that recognizes the wildness of the fire.
But the house is so big
it could be burning
(and you could be screaming)
for hours.

The urgency of common sense hits me like a tidal wave.
It says: *Get safe.*
It says: *Get gone.*

I want to watch, I tell you. *But I think we need to leave.*
I take a wobbly step toward the truck and reach for the keys
before I remember:
We are so damn drunk.

I don't want to die.
Here or on the road.
I'm too afraid to stay,
but more afraid to go.

Shit, I say, starting to freak out in earnest.
Shit shit shit.

And seconds before I'm about to scream or cry or fall to my knees,
thunder cracks
and I remember seeing the flickering, fire-like
lightning in the clouds.

The rain comes,
frozen and fast and furious,
spreading across everything
like safety.

Like a sudden savior.

64 DAYS BEFORE THE FIRE

After I stayed out past curfew totally by accident
(fell asleep in your basement, curled around you like a cat),
I was grounded.

I couldn't go out, but I could have company,
and you wanted to come over.

You wanted to come over, but ever since I'd gotten detention
because of the pervy gym teacher,
in-school suspension for giving the guy who called you a cow that
    bloody nose,
benched on the swim team because of the stink bomb,
my parents weren't your biggest fans.

It hurt you
that they didn't like you basically because of how much I did.
And I could have been kinder about that pain,
but I thought it didn't matter.
We were the ones who were friends (or whatever we were).
Why should we care what they, or anyone else, thought?

So you wanted to come over,
and I told you that you should,
and you asked if they'd be home
and I said yes.

I won't come, then, you said.

Why not?

I just can't.

They won't care.

But I could imagine how they might poke their heads into my room.
How there would be a split second of a frown before they smiled.
How you would notice.
How you might break.

How they might hover, might keep a close eye on us
(on you),
just to make sure we weren't doing anything "wrong."

And you didn't take kindly to being watched.

I'm not coming, okay?

But I want you to.

What about what I want?

I'm always thinking about what you want.

You didn't come.

I missed you.

And this became yet another complication
in the novel-length word problem
of us.

27. They are coming

I thought we were saved.

I look at you and you start smiling:
big cheeks and chattering teeth.
The rain is heavy and icy,
not quite snow, not quite sleet.
It blankets your hair in seconds,
making it fall like a damp, dark curtain —
the end of a play.

I grab your hand and open the truck door,
a bit of frigid shelter in the middle of the freezing storm.
You push me down,
climb on top.
Kiss me cold and hard,
your lips like ice.

The whiskey is working its warm magic in our blood,
and within seconds the ice in your hair is melting.
Rivulets run down your cheeks,
drip onto my neck and face and fingers.
New, soft rain that smells like you.

We sit up, look out at the house,
and it is still burning.
But the storm is doing its best wet work,
taming the flames.

We are inching closer and closer to safety.

But then we hear them:

sirens.

Only one at first and then more.
Someone must have seen the fire
licking the night sky like candy —
a psychedelic lantern in the dark.

Gimme your keys, you say.

    What? No.

I'm not as drunk as you.

    Yes, you are.

You grab for them.
I move away.
You try again, and I push open my door,
let them fly over the dirt and into overgrown, weedy grass.
It's too dark to see where they land.

You glare at me.
What the hell? Why would you do that?

    I'm not going to let you get yourself killed.

We can't drive.
It's too late to run.
We could try to hide, but they'd see my brother's truck.

It's in his name
and we both know what could happen to a Black man
whose truck is found at the scene of a crime.

They'd run his plates.
And even though the only tickets he's ever had
were a few parking ones *I* got,
they'd come for him.

It's all over, you say,
and I know you're right.

Fear shoots through me:
a silent, piercing scream.

I'm scared, but you're angry.
And the fire is doing something
to your already too-warm blood.
You climb back out of the truck,
back into the icy rain, and pick up a big rock.
You heave it toward the first floor,
shattering the one remaining unbroken window.
You scream again.

And then I'm yelling too,
like something feral needs to make its way out of my body.
I reach into your pocket, grab your lighter,
run the thirty feet to the next house.

I kick open the door.
Set tiny fires to all the garbage that covers the floor.
Because if we're going down,
let's hit the bottom like an anchor —
heavy and deliberate and digging in deep enough
to stop a whole ocean from shifting us,
to keep a giant ship from sailing away.

I run to the next house,
and the next one,
and the last one after that, lighting more mini fires and thinking,
Fuck it.
Fuck everything.
Fuck the whole world.

They are coming.
We are here.
There is nothing left to lose.

The fire trucks arrive first,
hoses flying,
water wailing.

Then the ambulances,
with kind paramedics who wrap us in blankets
that look like aluminum foil.

Then *they* come
with their badges and guns that are too often loaded;
too often happy to hurt people who look like us.
They try to smile, but we see right through their masks
to their real faces,
where fear hides behind anger,
where manners try to cover up
the looming, ever-present danger of their hands.

I am so afraid that I can't stop shaking.
And it's so bad the paramedics hand me another silver blanket
and then a paper cup of bitter coffee,
thinking I'm still cold.

What's your name, kid?
How old are you?
What about you?
Who drove?
Have you been drinking?
What happened here?
Do you know this is private property?
We're gonna have to take you down to the station.
You can call your parents from there.

The handcuffs are as cold as they are surprising.
The cop car is quiet except for the staticky voices on the radio.

The station is fluorescent bright.
The cell they put us in is filthy, but blessedly empty.

We never stop holding hands and all I keep thinking is:

No one cares
about those houses
until two Black kids
set them on fire.

You haven't said anything in far too long.

You okay? I ask,
and you shake your head hard, fast.

You still don't speak,
but inside I know you're screaming,
just like you did when you threw that rock.

I hope you never stop howling.

Lies:

"Love is blind."
"Time heals all wounds."

The truth?
Love can see just fine. But it's nearsighted.
Shortsighted.
And distance is the only thing that heals.

I had to get far away from you
and stay that way for a good, long while
to see anything about us
clearly.

But now I see.
Now I know.

You were never going to love me the way I needed to be loved.
      Without fear.
           Without hesitation.
                But with the kind of intensity that was as
                    hopeful as it was hopeless.

And how I loved you
(more than I'd ever loved anyone)
was not enough,
would never be enough.

I would have given you all of me.
But I could only love
as much of you
as you'd let me see.

38 DAYS BEFORE THE FIRE

You were yelling.
What do you want from me?

    I was whispering.
    Nothing. Just you.

What if I can't give you that?

    I'll still want it.

You'll never give up? Never let it go?

    Probably not, I said softly.

What if I'm already giving you all that I have to give?

    I didn't look away from you.
    Didn't even raise my voice as I said:
    I want more.

28. Your little friend

Underage drinking.
Trespassing.
Second- or, if we're lucky, third-degree arson.

These are the charges we leave with.
These are the words they hand us when our parents pick us up,
along with papers I don't understand — about court dates
and lawyers, probation and minimum sentences —
and a plastic baggie filled with the rings and bracelets
we had to take off before they took our prints.

My fingertips are still stained black.

My father is furious. He shouts the whole ride home.
My mother is silent, which is even scarier.

I don't even want to look at you, he says as we push open the door.
Get upstairs. I need to calm down. We'll talk in a few hours.

My mother still says nothing.

I'm almost at the top of the staircase when her voice finds me.

You are not to see her again, she says.

> *What?* I ask.

Your little friend.
You're not to see her again.

But Mama, this isn't her fault. We were just —

Why were you out of the house that late in the first place?
On a day when you'd already done something spectacularly stupid?

I was just making sure she was okay.

Mama sighs and says:
Exactly.
You're always chasing after her.
But have you ever stopped to ask yourself,
who is fighting for you?

I pause, ever so briefly,
swallowing my mother's words like poison:
Who is fighting for you?

You are reckless when it comes to her, she continues before I can
     speak.
Out of your mind.
I won't allow it.

The thing is,
if I wanted to see you, I could.
We go to the same school.

I know where you live.
Your folks are never home.

If I see that little girl's number on your phone again,
if she shows up on our doorstep or if I find out you've gone to hers,
if I so much as hear you say her name,
I will take your entire life away.

Parents think they control us with their authority.
But really the only reason we listen
is because we're desperate for them to love us.
And we're terrified that if we do too many bad things,
they'll stop.

So I do what I do best:
I lie.

I say okay.
That I won't see you.
That I won't talk to you.
That I'll leave you alone.

They take my phone.
Take my laptop.
Take the TV out of my room.
They say I can't leave the house except for school until my court
    date.
That I'll probably be grounded much longer than that, too.

But before they took everything away,
before we even left the station,
we agreed to meet at the bridge.

And if I really won't be seeing you for a while
(my throat feels tight even thinking about it),
there's no way I'm not going.

16 DAYS BEFORE THE FIRE

I let you cut my hair in your basement.

I sat on the concrete floor,
on the yellow stripe of the rainbow,
and stretched my legs across the green,
blue,
indigo,
and violet.

You sat on a red stool behind me,
your father's clippers buzzing —
a swarm of metallic bees in your hand.

You're sure? you asked.
I nodded.
You're sure you're sure?
I grinned.
I'm sure, I said. *Hair is stupid, unless it's yours.*
I don't want mine anymore.

I'd grown my hair out long
once or twice before.
But each time, I'd hated the weight of it,
the tickle of it against my neck and shoulders and back.

I've always loved long hair, but it took me a while to see
that I enjoyed it more on other girls
and hated having it all on me.

You cut slowly and carefully, brushing the bushy chunks
like dark cotton candy
from my shoulders to the floor.

You cupped my cheek to turn my head,
tapped my chin to tilt me back,
ran your fingers across my bare neck to brush tiny hairs,
like flecks of pepper,
off my skin.

When you were done,
you held up a mirror, and I looked like a different version of myself:
a truer, more free me.

My head's cold, I said.
It's literally perfect, you said.

You stroked my jawline with the backs of your fingers.
And it might have been the weed we smoked before you started the
     cut,
but I closed my eyes against the sensation
and my soul left my body.

Worth it? you asked.

And I would have shaved my head

a hundred thousand times

if you'd promised to touch me again in precisely that way.

I nodded.

A truth:

Maybe it was inevitable,
this falling together,
this falling apart.

But how long
could we
hold on?

29. There was love

We sneak out at dawn again
to meet at the bridge.
And I think it will be the way it always is.

I think I will say, *My parents went apeshit.*
I think you will say, *Mine too.*
I think I will say, *They told me I couldn't see you anymore.*
I think you will say, *Well, what they don't know won't hurt them.*
I think I will say, *How much should it be to get your parents off your*
     back?
I think you will say, *Maybe like three twenty-nine.*
I think I will take out my key. Add it to our menu.
I think we will kiss and toss stones
and watch the slowly rising, egg yolk–yellow sun.

But when I see your face, I can't say anything for five solid minutes.
You look like you just witnessed a murder.

         Are you okay? I finally ask.

I can't do this anymore, you say.

I take a step back.

I don't want to hear that.
I don't want to hear you.

I want to plug my ears, run away,
dive into cold, deafeningly deep water.

I touch my chest, feeling like it's betrayed me.
I didn't feel you the way I normally do.
I didn't see this coming.

  What? I say.

And you say it again. *I can't do this anymore.*

I cough out a laugh, because it is ridiculous.
Because I am choking on your words.
  What does that mean?

You swallow.
Maybe your throat is being scraped raw
by the absurdity of whatever you're talking about.

(I don't know what the hell you're talking about.)

It means we have to break up.

But how can you break up with someone who was never
(who was always)
yours?

  What? I say.

The horizon is turning purple, the beginning of a new day,
and I wish for perpetual darkness.
I wish for this night to never end, because in the light of tomorrow,
you will have said these words to me
and there will be no going back.
In the light of tomorrow,
I won't be able to pretend I was only dreaming.

I wish for yesterday
and all the days before yesterday
and all the days I've known you
and I even wish for the ones before I did,
because then I could look forward to meeting you.

I wish we were at the beach,
that it were just you the ocean and me,
so I could find my breath
in the rhythm of the beating waves.
So I could bury the broken pieces of us
in the sand.

I wish for a redo. An undo.
I wish you would shut the fuck up.

> *You can't dump me,* I say, all logic and shock.
> *You never even officially dated me.*

It doesn't matter, you say.
And then that sentence again,
the one I want to claw out of your throat with my fingernails:
I can't do this anymore.

I am so furious I can't breathe.

Do what? I ask defiantly,
not knowing exactly what you mean
(and knowing *exactly* what you mean).

If you're going to do it, you don't get to half do it.
If you're going to break my heart, and yours,
I'm going to make you fucking say it.

You know what, you say.

You can't kiss me anymore? I ask.
You can't be close to me anymore?
You can't talk to me anymore?

What exactly have we been doing that you just can't do
    anymore?

You sigh.
But that is not an answer.

    You can't hang out with me anymore?
    You can't hug me anymore?
    You can't text me anymore?
    Or will you still do those things but only when you *want to?*

Stop, you say.

    No. You can't do it anymore, right?
    So tell me what it is exactly that you can't do.

The pull and push has always been a part of us.
The running away. The coming back.
But I am only realizing, in this moment, that I haven't moved.
I've been standing right here,
loving you,
this whole time.

Any of it, you say. *I can't do any of it.*

    Why the fuck not?

Instead of answering my question, you say,
I . . . didn't think you would push back this much,
this hard.

And it hits like a lightning bolt, the mistake you made:
you mistook my softness
for weakness.

The truth is
I am infinitely powerful.

The truth is
I only surrendered to you because I wanted to.

The truth is
I love you
and there is strength in that, too.

But maybe there's too much unbridled power
in a love like ours
for someone used to holding it all in her own hands,
like you.

It's too much, you say, reading my mind.
And I want to punch you in the throat.
The feelings are too much. They overwhelm me.
And I want to tear this bridge down with my bare hands.
You are too much to take. We are too much for me to handle.
And I want to hold you and cry.

What happened? I ask.
What changed between the cop car and here?

Everything, you say.
Another non-answer.
Another disappointment.
Another reason for me to walk away.

But I don't.

This isn't the way we were supposed to end up, I say.
This isn't the way things were supposed to go.
I love you, I say, even though we don't say that,
because I don't know how to explain
that I plot detailed revenges for the people who have hurt
    you,
that if I think about you for too long it becomes difficult for
    me to swallow air.

Something inside me cracks.

I love you so much. Doesn't that matter?

Everything matters, you say, and you wrap your arms around your
    torso.
But it doesn't change anything.
I wish so much that it did.

The rim of the sky is punch-pink now,
streaked with pale tangerine and pure ocean blues.
But somehow, right above us, it is a deep indigo.
I can still see stars.

> *Fuck,* I say, and I feel sick.
> *Goddammit.*
> And my face is wet.

You step closer. And I push you, hard.
You stumble and fall, and I expect you to jump back up.
I almost want you to punch me in the gut,
in the chest,
in the face.
Body-slam me against the concrete.
Split my head open the way you've split my heart.

Maybe if we fight,
if we bruise each other in ways everyone can see
instead of in every single way they can't,
we can go back to being
us.

But when you don't move,
when you don't stand and hit back,
I drop to my knees to lift you up.
I examine your elbows and shins
for places I may have hurt you.

I'm sorry, I'm sorry,
I say and you say.
I'm sorry, forgive me,
I'm sorry, I love you.

We are holding hands
and we are on the ground
and we are crying.
And you are saying, *Shhh, shhh,*
and I am sobbing so much.
I am coughing and choking
and I keep wiping your face,
and I keep kissing your cheeks
and your forehead and your hair,
but my hands and lips are useless.
And you are cupping the back of my head
and I am trembling.
I am shaking so much
and you are holding me tight.

We are rocking back and forth,
clutching each other in this storm of our own making.
We are a tiny boat with torn sails,
unprepared for such turbulent weather.
The tears come as tempests,
falling quick and heavy like a summer hailstorm.
And it is still so dark that I want to start a fire.

But what difference would it make?
Nothing burns as bright as you.

We kiss.
Warm and wet and wildly.
And I can tell by the way you're touching me that you're serious.
You are desperate and deliberate and almost destructive.
You kiss me so hard that it hurts.
I can tell by the way we're devouring each other
that this is the end.
That you really mean it.
That you can't do this anymore.

Still, I want to remember you like this:
Slick-faced and honest.
Swollen-lipped, with curls glued to your cheeks by tears,
whispering, *I wish things were different.*
I wish love was enough.
I wish I knew what to do.
I wish it didn't hurt so much.
I wish, I wish, I wish.

Your eyes are dark and damp and I can't stop staring.

    Shhh, I say.
    It's okay.

It isn't okay,
(I'm crying so much I can't even breathe right)

but I need you to be okay.
So I will lie until you believe me.

Maybe, as hard as I tried to be good to you,
good for you,
maybe, I just wasn't.
Maybe, because we are opposites,
because I am me and you are you,
maybe, it always would have ended this way.
Maybe, my stubborn, hopeful heart whispers,
maybe, it won't be this way forever.

But it is this way right now.
And I have to find a way to live through it.
I have to find a way to go on existing if this is truly
the end
of us.

I kiss you, soft and slow.
And I want to fight for you, but I don't want to fight alone.

I'm worth fighting for too, I think,
remembering my mother's question.
And suddenly, I know it to be true.
I know it as well as I know my own name.
As well as I'll remember the curve of your bottom lip.
As well as I can imagine the ocean's deep, everywhere blue.

I am worth fighting for too.

You have been running away from me for years.
When all I ever needed,
all I ever wanted,
was for you
to stay.

When you stand up to leave this time, I let you go,
telling myself this is better for you.
This is what you need. This is what you want.
And all I've ever wanted was to give you everything you want.

So I let you go.
Even though losing you
is the worst thing
that's ever happened
in the history
of me.

*   *   *

I am not a poet.
But I have to write about us.
To prove that we were here.
To prove that it,
all of it
(all of us),
happened.

I take out my key.

We were here, I scratch into the metal of the bridge.
There was love.
It was messy
but it was real.

I'll hold these truths close to my chest
even as I vow to stay silent, from now on, about it all.

This knowing will have to be enough because
(and this truth hits me like a wrecking ball)

          that

          was

          our

          last

          kiss.

Before I tuck away the key, to drown stones like secrets
in the rushing water below, I write one more line,
thinking about how the word *stanza* means "room" in Italian
and how I'd build you a castle with my words if I could.

It is easy and true,
short and real.

I will never forget you.

5 DAYS BEFORE THE FIRE

Let's do something crazy, I said.
And you grinned.

30. No hard feelings

You turn around
right before you disappear.
Look back at me like you're remembering.
And the hope that rises in me is a phoenix:
fierce and flying, bright and burning.

I'm still sitting on the ground,
scratching reckless truths into the bridge,
the red paint flaking off like dried blood,
when you call out to me:

No hard feelings.

I want to grab you and kiss you again
and tell you this is stupid.
I want to hate you, now and forever,
but I don't. I won't.

We are wrong, so wrong.
Wrong for each other,
and most of the time
wrong about each other.
But there's something so right about us too.

(Right?)

I stand up. I take a few steps closer.

I look at your still fingers,
how far they are from mine.
I look at your tender, swollen eyes,
how they search for something,
anything,
other than me.
I look at your hips and your hair,
your lips and then at nothing but the air
all around us.

How much of it can slip between where I am
and where you are?
I remember how so recently we couldn't stand it —
any space between us at all.

How did we end up

                                                    here?

You used to ask me why I looked at your hands all the time.
It was because I wondered if you knew
how much of my heart was sitting right there
in the center of your palm,
your life line strung through it like a thread.

I wondered if you knew
how you could have crushed me with the loosest fist.
How quickly, easily, your long fingers and always painted nails
could have broken me in half.

(You had no idea.)

No hard feelings, you say,
and I think about your hair and the air,
your voice and your choice and your heart and my art
and my heart in your hands and your truths and my lies
and your hips and your lips and my eyes and your cries
and how I will always love you, every inch of you,
how the chemical equation of me plus you means
every atom of me is yours,
even if you grow to hate every molecule of everything
I've ever even touched.

I don't know how you don't see that I'm laid bare and barely
    breathing.
I don't know how you can think I could hold any of my feelings
    for you
anywhere except in the most delicate parts of my storm-tossed
    body.

The small of my back.
The underside of my wrist.
The hollow of my throat.
The inside of my cheek.

Losing you tastes salty and stings,
        like almost drowning.

It feels hot and desperate,
                    like leaving something vital
                    behind in a fire.

And when a gust of wind tosses the scent of your hair in my
        direction,
you smell the way you always do:
                    something sweet, burning.

But for once, I don't reach for you.
For once, when you run,
I don't follow.
For the first time
in the history of us,
I step
away.

I am worth fighting for too.

I decide I know the truth about me and you and us.
I've carved it into the metal of this bridge
and it is slashed into the meat of my heart.
Here the truth will live, permanent and perfect,
though we never were.

There was love. It was real. I will never forget you.

Worth it? I ask.

And what I mean is, was *I* worth it?

Were you?

Were we ever, since we aren't anymore?

I know my answer.

I don't wait for yours.

Instead, I say:

No. No hard feelings.

And as I turn my back to you,

I whisper,

Only the softest ones.

AFTER THE FIRE

I'm in the basement
alone
when I hear the front door open.
I wish for it to be you,
but I know it isn't.

I left you on a bridge,
scratching who knows what into wind-chapped metal,
paint being picked at until it falls away,
like old scales,
like scabby skin,
like everything that worked so hard,
bit by tiny bit,
to chip me away from you.

I hear footsteps
and I figure they'll move away from me
the way they always do.
My family is made up of ghosts,
but they're so *gone* my house doesn't even feel haunted.

Instead, the footsteps get closer.
I hear the basement door open.
And then my sister is suddenly there
in my space,
in my face.

What the hell happened to you? she says, eyes wide.
(My cheeks are on fire;
my tears only stoke the flames.)

Nothing, I say.
But what I mean is:
I love her and I've lost her.

Doesn't look like nothing, my sister says.

Well, it is, I say.
But what I mean is:
My chest is caving in.
My throat is closing up.
I cannot imagine a life without her.

We can talk about it, she says,
if you want.

When I look at my sister,
I realize I look just like her.
But we are nothing alike.

I am a bolt of lightning, while she is a cloudless night sky.
I am a clenched fist, while she is a hand with fingers splayed wide.
I am a crashing wave, violent rapids, a thundering waterfall;
she is a calm, wavering stream.

There are too many things about me that she will never understand.

No thanks, I say,
when what I mean is:
How does anyone survive
this?

Out of nowhere
she sweeps her thumbs across my cheeks —
soft skin, thin nails, warmth.
She spins her cold metal rings,
looks at me too closely and doesn't speak.

She moves closer.
She moves closer with too much tenderness.
I cover my mouth.
I close my eyes.

I break.

When my wet cheek lands in her lap,
I think of you.

(How long will I keep thinking of you?)

A lie (we'll tell ourselves until it becomes a truth):

"I don't love you anymore."

Author's Note

From as early as I can remember, I was told to be careful when it came to loving a boy. "Don't let him make a fool out of you."

"Don't let him break your heart."

"Make him work for it."

"Why buy the cow when you can get the milk for free?"

And so, with boys, I was always careful — with my body and with my heart. But with girls, I never was.

I have loved girls desperately.

I think it has something to do with not being taught to guard myself around them in the same way as I was conditioned to with boys. Girls are almost instantly and always vulnerable with other girls. We tell each other everything. We braid each other's hair. We sleep in each other's beds. We hold each other's secrets (and hands) gently and incessantly from the time we are very small.

That said, I didn't realize I was queer until the year I turned thirty. By then I had had several deeply intimate female friendships, and it was only in that moment — with hindsight, new language and understanding about queerness and attraction, and clarity about how ingrained bi-erasure is in our culture — that I was able to understand and dissect some of my intense and heavily romantic friendships with girls.

There is also this truth that has been bothering me more and more over the years, as I lost friend after friend and internalized it to mean something was wrong with *me* because no one likes to acknowledge it: there are people who are meant to be in your life temporarily, no matter how attached you become to them. I'd never seen a book that examined loving someone, wanting to hold on to them, but where the relationship was becoming untenable, not through the fault of either party. People can be incredibly compatible and fundamentally incompatible at once. And it can be earth-shattering, when all these things — friendship, romance, incompatibility — collide.

This book was born out of that.

So much goes into a successful relationship, whether it's platonic, romantic, or a messy mix of both. Timing and personality; a willingness to work for it; and love. Trauma and empathy and compassion and forgiveness. And with two girls, with that inherent and relentless vulnerability and closeness, all of that is ratcheted up even more.

I didn't have the insight I have now when I was younger. I'm not even sure I had it a year ago. But knowing what I know now, I wanted to write a book that showed that the end of a relationship doesn't mean you failed, or they failed, or you weren't meant to be. It just means you were meant to be for a time. And even when you get hurt, the feelings and experiences are still real and important and meaningful.

I have a deep appreciation for each time my heart was broken, and it's been broken many more times by girls than by boys. But with the boys, I never spoke to them again. With the girls, we held each other as we cried.

I hope this book can hold you as you cry the way writing it held me.

Acknowledgments

To Mommy:
For holding me close and keeping me safe,
even as I told you about an inexplicable love.

To Olivia:
For always listening, so well and so wonderfully.
For seeing my gold even when it is wrapped in blue.

To Marie:
For your brave and beautiful life.
For giving me the perfect title for this imperfect book.

To You:
For the mess you made of my heart.
For the truth I found in the wreckage.